"Are you okay?" Ashleigh ask~~ ... ~~here do you hurt?"

Melanie was disoriented. She didn't answer. She looked at Perfection. Samantha was on her knees in front of him, feeling his legs.

I should have listened to Dad and Christina, she thought. *I should have told Ashleigh. I'll probably be grounded for life!* Melanie wiped a hand over her face and watched as Perfection lifted his right foreleg in the air, refusing to put weight on it. Melanie turned her head into her aunt's shoulder and sobbed.

Now Perfection is hurt, she thought. *And it's all my fault.*

Collect all the books in the Thoroughbred series:

THOROUGHBRED Super Editions:

ASHLEIGH'S Thoroughbred Collection

*coming soon

THOROUGHBRED

ON THE TRACK

CREATED BY
JOANNA CAMPBELL

WRITTEN BY
LOIS SZYMANSKI

HarperEntertainment
A Division of HarperCollinsPublishers

HarperEntertainment

A Division of HarperCollins*Publishers*

10 East 53rd Street, New York, NY 10022-5299

17th
Street
Productions
A Division of Daniel Weiss Associates, Inc.

Produced by 17th Street Productions,
a division of Daniel Weiss Associates, Inc.

HarperCollins books are available at special quantity discounts
for bulk purchases for sales promotions, premiums, or fund-raising.
For information please write: Special Markets Department,
HarperCollins Publishers Inc., 10 East 53rd Street, New York, NY 10022–5299.

ISBN 0-06-106563-3

First printing: May 1999

Printed in the United States of America

Visit HarperEntertainment on the World Wide Web at
http://www.harpercollins.com

❖ 10 9 8 7 6 5 4 3 2 1

*To my dear friend, Shelley Sykes,
who shares my love of the written word*

ON THE TRACK

1

"ARENT YOU TAKING A LESSON WITH ME AT MONA'S today?" Christina Reese asked her cousin, Melanie Graham, as they walked down the gravel path from the house to the barns of Whitebrook Farm. The early autumn air was cool, and Melanie flipped up her jacket collar as she walked.

"No, I'm going to pony Faith this morning," Melanie said, "and hang around here today. Pirate needs the exercise, and it'll give Trib a break." She looked up at Christina as she talked. Although Melanie was a few months older, Christina was the taller of the two. "I'm just so glad it's Saturday."

"Me too," Christina agreed. "Sterling hasn't jumped for a week."

Keeping all the horses straight was fun for Melanie. Leap of Faith was Whitebrook's most promising race-

1

horse. Pirate's Treasure had been a track horse, too, before he'd lost his sight. Now Melanie used him to pony the horses in training to Whitebrook's practice track. Tribulation was Melanie's eventing pony. Trib had belonged to Christina before her parents had bought her Sterling Dream, a beautiful Thoroughbred.

Melanie loved this hour of the morning, just before the sun was fully up. The barns were bustling with activity as stalls were mucked out and horses were turned out to pasture. The ground was dusted with sparkling dew, and their footsteps left wet prints in the grass that would be melted away by the time the morning workouts on the track were over. The weather made Melanie think of the autumn ball that had been held a few weeks earlier at the Hunt Club's plantation house. She and Christina had worn vintage dresses they'd found in an old trunk in their friend Samantha Nelson's attic.

"One of these days we should get out your mother's old trunk," Melanie told Christina. "I want to see all her ribbons and trophies. That would be so cool!"

"We will, Mel," Christina promised. Her mother, Ashleigh Griffen, had been a famous jockey. She'd even been the first woman to win the both the Kentucky Derby and the Preakness, and she'd done it on Wonder's Pride, a horse she had raised herself.

At the entrance to the barn the pair parted ways, Christina to saddle Sterling, and Melanie to ready Pirate for the track.

"See you later," Christina called. "And don't forget we're all going out on a trail ride tomorrow."

"I wouldn't miss it!" Melanie shouted back as she waved good-bye.

Melanie hummed as she brushed Pirate Treasure's glossy black coat. A barn cat, purring contentedly, wove in and out of her legs while she worked. The lanky Thoroughbred didn't seem to mind the cat's presence. He leaned his head forward, ears pricked to listen, staring straight ahead. Since he'd lost his sight, Pirate's Treasure had learned to compensate by relying on his sense of smell and hearing. Melanie knew that people did that, but she was impressed that Pirate did it, too.

"You hear that old cat, don't you?" she asked, running her fingers along the horse's silky neck. Pirate shook his head at the whisper of breath in his ear when she spoke. Melanie leaned her head into his neck, breathing deep. It was a smell she never tired of. Horses were as much a part of Melanie as the sun and moon were part of the sky. And the warm smell of them always made her smile.

The gray striped tabby scrambled to the corner when a bucket rattled down the aisle. Melanie put the brushes and currycombs away and began to tack up Pirate. First she lifted the saddle pad over her head and onto the tall black's long back, carefully sliding it down and over the withers. Next came the smooth black saddle. She reached under Pirate's belly to pull the girth through and buckle it tight. Pirate lowered his head obediently when Melanie picked up the bridle. He accepted the bit as she pulled the straps up and over his ears, then reached to buckle the throatlatch.

She and Pirate had a relationship based on trust—neither had ever let the other down. Melanie thought back to when she lived in New York City and rode horses in Central Park. She had been involved in a tragic accident that killed her favorite horse. After that, Melanie had almost convinced herself that she and horses just didn't mix, that she could only do them harm. But Pirate had changed all that—he was blind and he trusted her.

The tabby cat shot out the stall door the second Melanie opened it. Melanie led Pirate out and down the long aisle, the clicking of his hooves echoing off the concrete in the cool walkway. She could see Leap of Faith standing with Samantha Nelson in the square of light just outside the barn. Samantha worked as a part-time trainer at Whitebrook while trying to get her own facility, Whisperwood, off the ground. Unlike Whitebrook, Samantha's farm focused on breeding jumpers and eventers, and she gave lessons to aspiring eventers. This morning she was with Whitebrook's exercise rider, Naomi Traeger, and the gray mare, Leap of Faith. Normally Melanie's aunt, Ashleigh, would be working with Naomi, but Ashleigh had been so busy that she'd asked Samantha to help her this morning.

4

Whitebrook was one of the best Thoroughbred breeding and training operations in Kentucky. Melanie often thought about how lucky she was that her aunt and uncle wanted her to live here with them. She missed her dad, who still lived in New York, but Whitebrook Farm was where Melanie was happiest.

Melanie picked up her pace. It took her eyes a moment to adjust to the light outside. Melanie smiled at Naomi and Samantha. "Think she'll run well today?" Melanie posed the same question every morning, no matter which horse Naomi was up on.

"Sure!" Naomi's dark hair framed her serious face.

"Enough small talk. Faith needs a run," Samantha said good-naturedly. As she talked, Samantha tugged gently on the stopwatch that hung from her neck. "Time to go."

Melanie clapped her riding helmet on her head and snapped the chin strap closed. She hooked a toe in her left stirrup and hoisted herself into the saddle, then turned to watch Samantha give Naomi a leg up. Samantha held Faith's reins in her left hand and cupped her right one under Naomi's knee. Naomi hopped up and down three times, then shot up into the saddle, landing lightly on Faith's back, settling gently. The mare sidestepped, rolling her eyes and blowing soft whuffs of air from her nostrils as she pranced. Each whuff created a small cloud of vapor that dissipated in the cool air. She was dappled dark and light gray with a black mane and tail. Although slightly shorter than

Pirate, she was a spitfire, always ready to go, a willing racer with a big career ahead of her.

Samantha handed Faith's lead up to Melanie and they turned toward the track in the distance. Melanie was sure they made a handsome pair, the tall black stallion calmly leading the slightly shorter gray mare with the prancing step and flashy head toss of a carnival horse.

Soft mist rose from the grass where sunlight touched it. Melanie waved when she saw Kevin McLean come out of the stallion barn, pushing a full wheelbarrow. Kevin didn't see her, though, and just kept to the business of stall cleaning.

Kevin was Samantha's younger half-brother. Their father was Ian McLean, Whitebrook's head trainer. Living at Whitebrook, Kevin couldn't help but love horses, too, and he and Melanie had become good friends. Maybe even more than friends.

Melanie turned her attention back to Faith, who walked complacently toward the track. Faith didn't really need a pony horse. She was all flash and high steps, but no real threat to her rider. Melanie knew that, but she loved to pony, and besides, it kept Pirate useful and in shape.

Samantha laughed. "Are you feeling pretty good today?" she asked Melanie as she walked along at Pirate's head.

Melanie felt confused. "Sure . . . but why do you ask?"

"The pink streaks!" Samantha explained.

Melanie reached up to pat the blond hair that peeked out from under her riding helmet. She'd dyed her hair the night before with cherry Kool-Aid. "Don't you like them?" she asked self-consciously.

"Sure. But you're like a mood ring. When there's pink in your hair, we know you're feeling pretty good. If it's blue, we know something's bothering you. Green . . . well, green means there's a real storm brewing!" Samantha exclaimed.

Naomi laughed, and Melanie blushed. It was true. Her hair color did depend on her mood, but she didn't think anyone else had noticed. She rubbed Pirate's mane and smiled.

They were almost to the track, and Samantha's demeanor showed it—suddenly she was all business. She turned to Naomi. "She's in good shape," she told the young rider, leaning into the filly's shoulder. "Take her out in an easy jog to the quarter pole. Then turn her for home and let her out full steam. Let's see what she's got in her today."

At the entrance to the track Melanie unsnapped the lead, and Faith broke into a steady jog, running counterclockwise on the track toward the red and white quarter pole. Melanie watched from Pirate's back, and Samantha propped her elbows on the rail, stopwatch in hand. They studied every move Naomi and Faith made, watching the rhythmic pumping of legs and the dirt that rose from the freshly raked track.

At the quarter pole Naomi turned Faith toward the wire and let her out. Faith's muscles rippled beneath her dappled gray coat. As her powerful body stretched out in a gallop, eating up the track, her hooves barely seemed to touch the ground. Melanie's heart raced. She could almost feel the wind in her face and taste the rising dust. Hearing the drumming hoofbeats, Pirate danced beneath her. *He wants to run,* Melanie thought. *He wants to be out there as much as I do!*

Faith bounded closer, legs pounding like pistons in an engine. As they shot under the finish wire Samantha clicked the stem down on the stopwatch. "Great!" she shouted, flashing a thumbs-up at Naomi. "She's prime today!"

Melanie mirrored Samantha's enthusiasm. "Uncle Mike told Aunt Ashleigh that Faith may just be Whitebrook's next big star!" she bubbled, her eyes alight.

"He could be right," Samantha agreed.

Melanie rubbed Pirate's neck vigorously. "You want to run, too, don't you, boy?" she said a little sadly, wondering if he knew he'd never be able to do that again. Then Melanie looked at Samantha and added, a little hesitantly, "I know how he feels—I want to race, too."

Melanie had loved horses as long as she could remember, but it wasn't until she came to Whitebrook Farm that she discovered what racing was all about. Pirate had caught her attention from the moment she first saw him. His spirit, like that of most racehorses, was full of fire. She'd fast become a part of the daily operation of the farm, and she'd come to love racing just as quickly. Ponying the Thoroughbreds and watching the other exercise riders had made her realize that she wanted to race, to be a jockey one day. She wanted it more than she'd ever wanted anything in her life, but this was the first time she'd told anyone her dream.

In the distance, Naomi had stopped Faith and turned her to the inside of the track. The mare was itching to run and would go tearing off for the barn given half a chance. As they waited Samantha broke the silence. "You know, Mel, it's not too early for you to start training as an exercise rider." She hesitated. "I mean, if that's what you want to do."

Melanie flushed. *If* that's what she wanted to do! For Melanie, there was no doubt. She not only wanted to do it, she ached with the desire. She gulped and nodded, pink and blond hair bobbing. "Yes, it's all I want to do," she gasped.

Samantha twisted the cord of the stopwatch in her hand as she spoke. "I'd have to ask Ashleigh first, but I could get you up on some horses, if you want," she suggested.

"That would be great." Melanie tried to contain her excitement, but her voice came out in a squeak.

"Good," Samantha agreed. "I'll talk to Ashleigh later this morning when we go over the workout."

Samantha walked toward Naomi and Faith, who were leaving the track at a controlled jog. She handed

Melanie Faith's reins as Naomi dismounted, and Melanie began to lead Faith back to the barn.

Behind her, Melanie heard Naomi and Samantha discussing the workout and upcoming plans for Faith, but she wasn't really listening. She could hardly believe it. *Soon I'll be riding racehorses,* she thought.

When they reached the barn, Naomi took Faith's reins and led the mare into the wash rack to hose her off. Samantha headed down the aisle to look for Ashleigh.

"I'll see you in a few minutes," Melanie called, turning Pirate down one of the grassy paths between the paddocks. She pushed him into a trot. He needed a little exercise, but even more, Melanie needed to be alone to digest her excitement. The breeze on her face and the steady beat of Pirate's hooves on the path helped her relax.

After Pirate was untacked and turned out in the paddock, Melanie wandered over to the broodmare barn. She wanted to see Kevin and tell him her exciting news, but Kevin had left the barns for the day. She looked in on each mare. At the end of the row she stopped to talk to Perfect Heart. The chestnut mare was heavy with foal. Melanie knew how much everyone at Whitebrook was banking on this one. The father was Pride's Chance, one in a line of fine foals Wonder's Pride had sired. Perfect Heart milled around in her stall, nosing the golden straw at her feet. Maybe Heart wasn't used to having so much straw—the horses got extra bedding during foaling time. Or maybe the mare was just restless. Heart pawed a few moments more, then stood, her head down, while Melanie stroked the white heart shape that graced her forehead. The mare moved closer as Melanie stroked, her head resting against Melanie's left arm while she stroked her with the right hand. Gradually the mare's eyes closed, and Melanie left her standing in the stall, dozing.

The sun had gone behind a cloud and a slight breeze had kicked up, as though a storm was threatening. Melanie hurried up the drive to the rambling farmhouse.

Inside the house, Melanie raced upstairs to Christina's room. Her cousin was sprawled on the carpeted floor in front of her tiny television, watching a video of herself and Sterling riding in an event. She was so engrossed in the video that she didn't hear Melanie come in.

"I remember that event," Melanie said, watching over Christina's shoulder. The video was from the previous summer, when the girls had gone to riding camp together.

"Can you believe how much Sterling and I have learned in just a few months?" Christina asked. "I mean, look at the way I let her rush that jump. Jeez!"

"Hmmm." Melanie glanced at the screen. "You have come a long way," she agreed.

"You would, too, if you'd take your jumping lessons more often," Christina chastised.

"Oh, Chris, you won't believe this," Melanie said, and sank down on the bed. She could hardly contain the excitement in her voice. "But if things work out the way I want them to, I won't be taking as many lessons at Mona's," she added.

Christina clicked off the television set. "What are you talking about?" she demanded.

Melanie's eyes danced. She stood up and began to pace as she talked. "Samantha said she could put me up on some of the racehorses," she explained. "She said it wasn't too early to start training to be an exercise rider!" Melanie spun around and dropped back onto Christina's bed. "Can you believe it?" she cried, looking at her cousin upside-down from the bed.

"That's what you want to do? What about jumping and eventing?" Christina asked, gazing down at her.

Melanie sat up to face her cousin. "I think I'm going to like flat racing more. There'll still be time for trail rides and stuff. But I really want to do this." Melanie liked riding at Mona's farm, but if she took time away from her morning barn work to exercise-ride, she'd have to do the barn work in the evening and find time for homework, too. "Anyway, maybe I'm jumping the gun," she said. "Sam says she has to talk to your mom first, to make sure it's okay with her." Melanie paused. "Do you think she'll let me?"

Christina stared at her hands and shrugged. "Yeah. She'll love it," she said quietly.

Melanie slid to the floor and sat down next to

12

Christina. She flung an arm around her cousin, sweeping Christina's long hair to one side. "Don't worry, Chris. I'll still be around enough to annoy you!"

"I know," Christina said slowly. "You'll probably love being an exercise rider, but it's going to take up all your free time." Christina looked sad. "This is my last week of taking lessons at Mona's," she said. "I start with Samantha at her farm next week." She hesitated, then added, "I'm going to miss everyone."

"Yeah, but Samantha's so great," Melanie said. "And Mona's too protective of you—she told you that herself. It'll be good for you to take lessons from someone else."

"I know." Christina sighed, twirling her strawberry blond hair on an index finger. "But I'll miss Mona. She's been my teacher for eight years—she's like my second mom."

Melanie nodded, trying to understand.

"Hey, are you coming on the trail ride tomorrow?" Christina asked her.

"Of course. I wouldn't miss it for the world," Melanie promised.

Christina looked thoughtful. "My mom was hoping I would want to learn to exercise-ride," she said slowly. "But I never really got into it." She hesitated. "I think I kind of let her down. . . . Anyway," she continued, jumping up, "I have to get some work done in the barns."

"Want help?" Melanie offered.

"No. I'm just going to clean some of the tack that's getting ratty-looking. But thanks," Christina added.

Melanie stared after her. Did Christina mind that she was learning to exercise-ride?

Dinner at Whitebrook was usually an enjoyable family time, a time Melanie looked forward to. But this evening she was apprehensive. Had Samantha talked to Ashleigh? And if she had, what did Ashleigh say? Would Melanie be allowed to ride on the track?

"So, Melanie, Samantha told me you're interested in helping exercise the horses," Ashleigh announced once everyone was seated. "And I think it's great!" Bowls of mashed potatoes, gravy, fried chicken, and beans were circulating. Ashleigh waved a fork at Melanie. "If you like it and you're good at it, you could become a jockey one day. You have the right build, you know," she said emphatically.

Melanie grinned. Next to her, Christina put down her glass.

"Christina, did you tell Mel we once talked about you learning to exercise-ride?" Ashleigh asked.

"Yes," Christina answered hollowly.

"It was something Chris never really wanted to do," Ashleigh said. "And now she turned out to be so good at eventing."

Christina nodded. "I'll probably grow too tall to be a jockey, anyway." She twirled her fork in her plate, then laid it down. "May I be excused?" she asked, and slid her chair back.

"Of course, honey. Are you sure you've had enough to eat?" Ashleigh said, furrowing her brow.

"Yes," Christina said over her shoulder as she left the room. Melanie watched her disappear, with the nagging suspicion that something was wrong.

Later that evening Melanie was in the barn with Pirate when she heard footsteps outside the stall.

"Mel, it's me!"

It was Kevin. "In here," Melanie called.

"I should have known." Kevin popped his head over the stall door and smiled. "What do I have to do to win your heart away from that old black horse?"

Melanie was used to Kevin's jokes, so she ignored the question and answered with a question of her own. "Did you hear?" she asked. "I'm going to learn to exercise-ride."

"I know," Kevin said, nodding. "My sister told me all about it. She said Ashleigh is pretty excited about it, too."

"Really?" Melanie suddenly felt giddy. Ashleigh was excited about her learning to exercise-ride? "What else did she say?"

Kevin's wavy reddish hair reflected the overhead lights, and his freckles faded into the ruddy sunburn that stretched across his nose. "Just that you seem to want this a lot," he said, a smile playing on his lips.

Melanie leaned into Pirate's neck. "I do, but Chris is a little worried. She says it's going to take up all my time, and I already miss too many lessons at Mona's. I think she's also worried that we won't be able to hang out as much," Melanie added thoughtfully.

"Just let Mona know that you'll be riding at White-brook for a while," Kevin reassured her. "And don't worry. Chris will be okay."

"Yeah, I guess," Melanie answered. But she wasn't so sure.

2

MELANIE COULD NOT SLEEP. MIXED EMOTIONS SWIRLED inside her, and she didn't know whether to feel happy or sad. Christina hadn't said much all evening, and Melanie wondered what was going on in her cousin's mind. At the same time, Ashleigh had said she could start her training the next day, and Melanie was so excited about riding that she could burst. She tried to curl on her side to sleep, but her eyes just popped open again. *Maybe some hot chocolate would help*, she thought. She crept downstairs, flicking on lights in the hall and then the dining room as she passed through. She was surprised to see the dim glow of the kitchen light and Ashleigh sitting at the kitchen table, bent over a pile of papers.

"What are you doing up?" Ashleigh asked when she saw Melanie come in.

"I was just about to ask you the same thing," Melanie said to her aunt.

"I'm working on some figures," Ashleigh said. She had the blue farm book spread out before her, the one with each horse listed inside. Melanie knew it held records of the expenditures and the income garnered from each horse. "I'm trying to decide which yearlings will go to the yearling sale. It's tough. They all seem to be on a level playing field this year. There's not one that stands out above the rest. But who knows?" Her voice trailed off. "Maybe next year's crop of foals will be better."

"They will," Melanie said brightly. "You'll have Perfect Heart's foal—Pride's bloodlines won't let you down." She opened a cabinet and pulled out a saucepan, then opened the refrigerator door.

Ashleigh paused, sticking the pencil behind her ear and stretching her arms above her head. "You're right," she agreed. "Pride never lets us down." Her gaze focused on Melanie, who was pouring milk in the saucepan. "So, you never did tell me. What are you doing up this late?" she repeated.

"I couldn't sleep. I thought some hot chocolate would help," Melanie explained. "Would you like some?"

"Nope. But thank you," Ashleigh said, and shut the farm book firmly. "Some decisions can wait until morning. Why couldn't you sleep?" she asked, smiling. Melanie felt certain her aunt knew the feelings that bubbled inside her. "Excited about riding in the morning?"

"Definitely," Melanie answered solemnly. She didn't mention Christina or the worry that filled her over her cousin's mood change. With the yearling sale coming up in just three weeks, Aunt Ashleigh had enough to worry about.

"Well, don't worry." Ashleigh stood up, yawning. She put her arm around Melanie. "You don't have any reason to be afraid," she said, smiling. "We're going to put you up on Heart of Stone, and he's as solid as they come. Besides, you know what you're doing. I've watched you ride. You'll be great." Ashleigh yawned again. "I've been up since five-thirty this morning, or yesterday . . . whatever. I have to get some sleep," she said. She gave Melanie a squeeze. "I am so pleased that you're doing this," she said. "It means a lot to have family interested in racing."

Melanie beamed. Then she heard a noise behind them and turned to see Christina standing in the kitchen doorway in her pajamas. *How long has she been standing there?* Melanie wondered.

"Hi, Chris. Did you have trouble sleeping, too?" Ashleigh asked.

"Yeah," Christina responded, rubbing her eyes and leaning against the door frame.

"I'm making some hot chocolate. Want some?" Melanie offered.

Christina hesitated.

"Have some," Ashleigh insisted. "It might help you sleep. And maybe you can talk Melanie out of her nervousness." On her way out, Ashleigh hugged Christina goodnight.

Christina stood in the doorway a moment after her mom disappeared down the hallway.

"I'll get the hot chocolate," Melanie offered.

"No, thanks," Christina said, sweeping her hair back. "I think I'll go back to bed," she said quietly, and headed for the stairs.

After she'd gone, Melanie stirred a packet of cocoa mix into a mug of warm milk. She sat at the table staring into the marbled brown liquid. The clock on the wall ticked loudly as she sipped from her cup. She wondered again if Christina had heard what her mother said to Melanie.

Melanie stirred the hot chocolate one more time, then lifted it to sip. It was warm and comforting. She swished it in her mouth and wondered if Christina was okay.

As the clock ticked and Melanie sipped her chocolate to the bottom of the cup, she heard Ashleigh's words again in her head. It felt good to have something in common with Ashleigh. She just hoped she didn't let her aunt down.

When Melanie dragged herself groggily to the barn early Sunday morning, she heard two voices coming from the stall at the very end of the aisle. She stopped to pat Pirate, giving him a scratch behind the ears before moving on. As she drew closer she recognized the voices as Samantha's and Ashleigh's.

"I can't tell you how happy I am that Melanie wants to do this," Ashleigh said. "Not just because she's doing what I love, but because I believe it will be good for her, too."

"Didn't you think at one time that Christina would want to do some exercise riding?" Samantha asked.

"Yes, but she never really got into it," Ashleigh remembered out loud. "Of course, I always hoped she would. . . ." Ashleigh's voice trailed off.

"Yeah, but that girl sure can ride," Samantha responded.

"Christina says she wants to go to the Olympics in eventing. I think she has it in her, too," Ashleigh remarked.

"So do I," Samantha agreed. "I've seen her take Sterling through courses that mare was determined not to do. They have a connection. I just hope Chris realizes her own talent."

Ashleigh sighed. "I try to let her know she's good, but I don't know if she hears me. After all, I am her mother."

Samantha chuckled.

Melanie heard a rattle, then Ashleigh added, "I sure hope Melanie sticks with it. She has everything it takes: drive, determination, and good horse sense."

21

Samantha looked up as Melanie approached. "There you are, Mel," she called out. "Ready?"

Melanie gulped and nodded. "What's the plan?" she asked. She was still glowing from her aunt's remarks. She didn't know Ashleigh had given much thought to her riding skills.

"Well," Samantha said, "Stone's all ready to go."

Ashleigh smiled at Melanie. "Today's your day, Mel," she said, opening Stone's stall door.

Stone's dark bay coat shone in the early morning light, and his black ear tips and muzzle looked like velvet. Ashleigh led him out of the stall and snapped the crossties hanging from the wall onto his halter. Samantha picked up the tiny racing saddle that rested on the saddle rack outside his stall. She threw a pad over his back, smoothed it down, and slipped the saddle on. A moment later he was bridled and Samantha was leading him outside. They stopped to gaze at the track in the distance.

"Is Naomi coming today?" Melanie asked.

"No, she has the day off," Ashleigh explained. "She said to wish you luck on your first ride, though."

It really wasn't her first ride, far from it. But it was her first time out on the track—something a little scary, but totally awesome.

Samantha twisted her stopwatch. "Nervous?" she asked.

"A little," Melanie admitted.

"You don't have to be. Ashleigh and I talked about

it and decided to go easy on you." She grinned.

"Stop it, Sam," Ashleigh said, but she was smiling. Her expression turned serious when she began to give advice to Melanie. "Stone's not our fastest horse, but he could be," she said. "He runs hot or cold. One day he's really on top of it, into it, ready to run, his heart on the track. The next day he's lazy—his attention isn't on the job at hand." She shook her head. "He's not consistent. And right now we don't know what we're going to do with him. You can ride him for us until we decide. We're going to try some different training tactics, if you're up to it."

Melanie scrunched her forehead in concentration, taking in everything Ashleigh had to say. "Sure."

Ashleigh touched Melanie's shoulder. "You don't have to worry, though. He's a good, solid horse," she assured her. "He won't run away with you or anything. That's the main reason we're starting you on him."

"I'm not worried." Melanie patted Stone as she spoke, finger-combing the strands of the black forelock that spilled over his forehead.

"Let me give you a leg up." Samantha cupped her hand, and Melanie did her best to imitate Naomi's move from the day before, hopping a few times before putting force into her jump. Stone was a little taller than Pirate, and the saddle was a lot smaller than the regular English saddle she was used to. She didn't make it all the way up, but scrambled for a moment to pull herself up the rest of the way. She put her feet in the stirrups. Her knees seemed too high, though she knew the position was right. It would take some getting used to, but it kept her weight distributed better so Stone's run would not be affected. She knew that jockeys wore their stirrups even higher.

Samantha took Stone's bridle and they walked toward the track. Melanie was flying high. With each swaying step Stone took, her mood became lighter. It felt so right to have the big bay under her, his powerful shoulder muscles rippling beside her knees. Melanie marveled at the differences she felt. With Trib, her stirrups were long and her legs were down. Trib's walk was bouncy and his pony trot was even bouncier. Pirate had the longer Thoroughbred stride, but even he did not feel the same. She didn't perch on his back, knees high, but rode with her legs wrapped around his barrel, sitting deep in the saddle.

"Concentrate on keeping him in check this morning," Ashleigh said, and looked up at Melanie as she spoke. "Depending on his mood, he may want to run. But we don't want that from him today. We're letting him smell the candy, but promising it to him for later. Let him think about the run, let him want the run, but hold him in. Here—I'll show you how to wrap the reins around your hands so he can't pull them loose."

Ashleigh demonstrated, wrapping the reins around her clasped hand. Then she handed the reins back to Melanie and watched as she wrapped them around her small fists. "Even if he jerks away, you still have leverage. If you want to let him go a little, just let out the last wrap," Ashleigh explained.

Melanie held her hands in place. It seemed easy enough, but she knew it would be different once they were galloping.

When Ashleigh paused, Samantha added, "Take your time getting to know him. We want you to feel how he feels and think like he thinks before we let him go full steam with you."

Melanie nodded. She knew just what they were talking about because she had that kind of relationship with Pirate. She knew how the big black was feeling most of the time, and she knew it without even trying. She looked down at Stone and concentrated on trying to feel his mood. But all she felt were the big swinging steps that pulled them closer to the track.

The misty dew had been burned away from any grass the sunlight had touched, but the shaded areas glimmered as though they were covered with so many tiny diamonds. By the time the run was over, Melanie knew the sun would be full up. She was happy it was Sunday and she wouldn't have to rush off to school after the workout.

Just outside the gate they stopped. "No starting gate yet," Ashleigh said, and Samantha raised her eyebrows. "He's getting gate-sour, acting up inside," she answered Samantha's look, "and I want to start Mel slow." She looked thoughtful. "Maybe less work in the starting gate will get Stone's mind back on the race, where it belongs."

Melanie was relieved—she'd never broken a horse from the gate before. She looked down, waiting for more instructions.

"We want you to take him out just the way you saw Naomi do yesterday," Samantha said. "Jog him to the quarter pole. But stop him there and make him face the inside of the track. Let him know that you are in charge and that you'll decide when it is time to go."

Melanie nodded.

"When you feel he's ready, and you're ready, turn him toward the wire and let him out in a slow, easy gallop. Let the reins give and take with his strides. I know you've done that with Tribulation riding cross-country courses, but you'll see the difference with Stone. His strides are huge, and he'll need more rein. Just a hand gallop," she said again.

"Okay." Melanie reached a gloved hand up to check her chin strap and to wipe a bead of sweat from under the edge of her helmet. It sounded easy enough, but butterflies were flitting about in her stomach.

"He's all yours." Ashleigh beamed. "Enjoy it."

Melanie leaned forward as Stone stepped onto the track. She felt his pace quicken, and her heart followed suit. She leaned forward and squeezed with her knees, letting him out slowly, and he broke into the easy jog she wanted, his mouth light on the bit.

Stone's strides were long, and she settled into them

quickly, enjoying the breeze in her face and the smell of wet clay that rose from his pounding hooves. Already the position that had at first seemed so strange to Melanie now felt more comfortable. Her knees were where they should be. When she stood up in the stirrups and leaned into Stone's neck, he jumped a gear, moving slightly faster. His mane was like soft wispy feathers brushing her chin as she watched the track ahead, looking between two pricked ears. She could feel Stone's excitement, and it coursed through her, too, as the track became a blur beneath them.

Melanie could see the quarter pole ahead and began easing Stone in, gathering the reins between her fingers, feeling him respond beneath her. He slowed, dropping into a swinging walk just before they reached the red and white striped pole. She stopped him there and turned him to face the inside of the track. He fought her some, prancing under her like a bundle of hot wires, sidestepping to the right. Melanie gathered her reins tighter and used pressure from her right leg to swing him back into line, talking to him all the while. "Easy there, boy. We'll go in a minute. Easy, Stoney boy," she crooned.

A fine line of sweat had broken out over Stone's shoulders, and Melanie reached down to wipe it away. "Easy," she told him. "Easy, boy."

Stone settled, looking at the grassy oval inside the track, but his head swung to look down the track again and again, and Melanie could feel he wanted to go.

The time was right—he knew she was in control, but the longing to run was there. Melanie turned the big horse and gave him the go-ahead. As soon as he felt the reins loosen and her legs tighten, he broke into a trot. She gave him more rein and he took it, his strides lengthening into a canter, then a gallop. Melanie badly wanted to let him run with all his heart, to feel what it was like. Her own heart was keeping time with his pounding hooves, but she followed Samantha's and Ashleigh's instructions, knowing it was best to keep to his training program. She was standing in the stirrups, Stone's body pumping below her, the warm smell of horse, earth, and morning dew flowing through her. Before she knew it they were flying under the wire and she was pulling him up, letting him jog around the track as he slowed. Exhilaration filled her. When she reached down to pat Stone's neck, he dropped his pace again. She turned him, and he fell into a walk. Together they swung down the track toward Samantha and Ashleigh.

Samantha was smiling broadly, and Ashleigh was practically jumping up and down. "Way to go, Mel," Ashleigh yelled with a wave. She was smiling all over. "I told you she'd be good," she told Samantha. "She's a natural!"

Melanie beamed down at them from atop Heart of Stone. She rubbed his mane and patted his neck. "Good boy," she said. "Good boy!" She felt proud, and grateful that Stone had responded to her so well. After all, Stone had done the hard part. She looked at Ashleigh and Samantha and then down at Stone. Galloping on the track was so much fun. How could she have lived without it? *I never will again*, she promised herself.

Sam led them off the practice track and they made their way back to the barn. Behind them, Melanie saw Christina, watching from Sterling's back. The elegant gray mare held her head high. Sterling was beautiful and always carried herself proudly.

Melanie waved, and Ashleigh turned to look.

"Good morning, sweetie!" Ashleigh yelled. "Did you see Mel go?"

"Hi, Mom," Christina called.

She lifted her hand in a halfhearted wave and turned to ride in the opposite direction, ignoring Melanie altogether.

"Hey, Chris!" Melanie shouted after her.

"I'm late for my last lesson at Mona's," Christina called back as she squeezed Sterling into a trot and rode away.

3

IN SPITE OF CHRISTINA'S SLIGHT, MELANIE FELT AS THOUGH she were floating on a cloud. The rest of the day she worked in the barns until late afternoon, stopping only for a quick lunch. She bathed and hand-walked Stone to get to know him better. She put him in crossties and groomed him, rubbing his legs down with liniment and talking to him all the while. Then she moved down to Pirate's stall. She'd have to work extra hard to make sure he didn't feel neglected. She groomed his black coat until it shone with a purple glow, and the white star on his forehead stood out in stark contrast.

Melanie was so excited about her training she wished she could call her dad and share her excitement with him. But Will Graham was a record producer, and his job had taken him to England to promote a big act he'd just signed. She knew he wouldn't be home for a few days. So she basked in her own joy while she picked the manure and wet spots from both stalls and then went to visit the broodmares.

Perfect Heart was still pawing at the straw in her box stall from time to time, but the foal had not dropped back, the milk bag was not full, and the skin over her rump had not loosened up. Those would have been signs that the foaling would take place within the week. Without those signs, Melanie knew there was still a wait ahead.

By the time the late afternoon sun had dropped low over the barns at Whitebrook, Melanie was ready for a shower. She thought she would run into Christina in the house and they could talk, but her cousin was nowhere in sight.

Melanie stood in the shower, letting the warm water sluice over her tired muscles. She hadn't realized how worn out she was until she had finally stopped. *This training is going to be a lot of work,* she realized, *but the best kind of work.* Then she groaned. *Tomorrow is Monday,* she thought, realizing she'd have to figure out a way to squeeze riding, school, and homework into her schedule. She stayed in the shower until the steam was so thick the mirrors ran like spigots. Then she stepped out, wrapped a towel around herself, and returned to her bedroom, where she plunked down on the bed. She lay back and closed her eyes, trying to think clearly. She practiced what she would say to Christina when she saw her. She'd just ask her flat out, *What's wrong? You've been acting kind of strange. Are you mad at me or something?*

Slowly, Melanie rose and slipped into a pair of shorts and a T-shirt. Her dirty jeans and chaps were in a pile on the floor, but she didn't care. She was too tired to clean up. She padded down the hall to Christina's room to see if they could talk. The room was still empty. Melanie sat down on Christina's bed and flicked on the television. The video was still in the player, and it came on. Melanie lay on the bed and watched Christina and Sterling Dream rounding the ring in a competition. Together they took a cross rail, then a wall, followed by an oxer. *They're good*, Melanie thought. *They're better than good.* Christina had brought Sterling so far, even moving her up from novice level to training level in the last show. The video was still playing when Melanie's eyes drifted shut and she fell asleep on the bed.

She awoke with a start. Christina was standing over her, staring. Melanie pushed herself up on an elbow, trying to focus. "Hi, Chris," she mumbled, yawning.

"Hey," Christina said, and reached over to flick off the television. "Sleeping in the middle of the day? On my bed?"

"Yeah. I was waiting for you, and I was kind of tired," Melanie explained, grinning sheepishly. She was about to ask Christina what was bothering her, but before she could, Christina interrupted.

"You'd have seen me if you had come to Mona's," she finally said. "It was my last lesson there, and I kind of thought you might come after your workout on the track." She paused. "Everyone wanted to know why you didn't. Katie and Kevin and Dylan and Cassidy were all there. And Mona said you wouldn't be taking any lessons for a while."

Melanie swallowed. "What did you say?" she asked.

Christina shrugged and sat down in her desk chair. "I told them that you'd rather work here with the race-horses," she explained.

Melanie sat up, sitting cross legged in the middle of the bed, and stared at Christina. "That's not how it is, Chris. You know that." She hesitated, trying to gather her thoughts. "It was so awesome. I've never felt anything like it—Stone galloping so fast. You should know how it feels to want something that much. I love it, just like you love eventing."

Christina stood up, her feet hitting the floor with a clunk. "Yeah, I guess. But I hope training to be an exercise rider doesn't mean you'll forget your friends." She shrugged again and started out the doorway.

Melanie winced. *Where did that comment come from?* she wondered.

Then Christina stopped. "By the way," she said, turning around, "you missed the trail ride."

"Oh, my gosh!" Melanie shouted, and thumped herself on the head. "I completely forgot! Hey, Chris!" she yelled as Christina started to walk away. "It won't happen again, I promise. I can keep up with our friends, and school, and exercise riding, too."

"I hope so," Christina called back, but it sounded as if she didn't believe it at all.

Melanie swung her legs off the side of the bed. Why did Christina have to say it like that? Melanie wasn't about to forget her good friends. She thought about her other riding friends—Dylan Becker, Katie Garrity, and Cassidy Smith. They'd had a lot of fun over the summer, and more recently at the hunt club event. Then she thought about Christina, and remembered that she'd never even gotten around to asking her what was bothering her. A wave of sadness washed over her. She wondered if Christina was jealous of the attention she was getting from Ashleigh. Christina would never admit it, and Melanie had no idea what to do if it turned out to be true.

Over the next week Melanie fell into a routine of training. She was up before the sun and in the barn grooming. By the time the first rays of morning light peeked over the hilltop, reflecting brightly off the roofs of Whitebrook's barns, Melanie was on the track with Stone beneath her and Ashleigh or Samantha at her side, and sometimes Samantha's and Kevin's father, Ian, too. What a thrill! She was getting to know Stone's personality better and better, and he was learning her quirks as well. Each morning after the workout she hurried into the house to shower and head off to school.

In the evenings she did her barn work and rode Pirate to keep him in shape, then did homework until late. Sometimes she and Christina did their homework in the dining room together. They talked, but Melanie felt Christina distancing herself. She often saw Christina ride off toward Samantha's farm, Whisperwood, for eventing lessons there.

On Friday Melanie hurried home from school. Even Christina's attitude couldn't dull her happiness. School would be closed for a five-day weekend, and Melanie was looking forward to all the extra time she would have with the horses.

Saturday morning Ashleigh was particularly bubbly when they met in the barn for the morning workout. "Does Stone feel like your partner yet?" she asked.

Melanie was wrapping Stone's front legs. She answered without hesitation. "Definitely. I can almost feel what he's going to do next. I think he knows me pretty well, too."

"That's what I thought. Samantha and I think you're ready to let him full out on the track today."

"Full gallop?" Melanie asked, excitement taking over as she stood up and took Stone's reins.

"Yes," Ashleigh said, smiling. "If you're game," she added.

Samantha joined them with the saddle over her arm. "We've watched you closely this week, and we think you can handle him. How do you feel about that?" She placed the saddle pad and then the saddle on Stone's back.

"I'm ready!" Melanie grinned at her aunt, then at Samantha. "Stone's ready, too!" she said, patting the dark bay horse, who snorted in response.

"All right, then." Ashleigh walked beside Melanie, who had her riding helmet tucked under her arm. The three of them led Stone out of the barn. "You really remind me of myself at your age," Ashleigh told Melanie. Then she ruffled Melanie's hair, flipping an orange streak playfully. "Except for this, of course!"

Melanie smoothed down her hair and pushed the helmet down on her head. "I guess not many jockeys have streaks in their hair," she quipped, but she was thinking about how good it felt to be compared to her famous jockey aunt.

When they reached the track, the sun was glinting off the silver ball that held the weather vane on top of the stallion barn, as if offering a promise for the run ahead. Melanie leaned into Stone's dark bay shoulder, and he lowered his neck. "We're going to have a great run," she told him, and he tossed his head playfully, trying to shake her breath out of his ear.

"Up you go," Samantha said as she offered a cupped hand for a leg up.

Melanie settled in the saddle, gathered her reins,

36

and waited for instructions. Stone was prancing. He felt a difference. Melanie was already communicating her anticipation and excitement, and Stone was picking up on it.

Melanie saw Naomi and Faith come off the track with Ian walking just behind. Ian was grinning from ear to ear. "Faith just put in a great time," he told Ashleigh.

"Good," Ashleigh said enthusiastically. "How's Naomi looking?"

"Better than ever. She's ready," he said, and Melanie wondered if he was talking about Faith or Naomi.

Naomi had dismounted and was walking Faith toward the barn.

"I'll meet you in a little bit," Ian called after her. "I want to catch Melanie's run."

Naomi raised her hand in a wave.

Ashleigh turned to Melanie. "Jog him out to the quarter pole, like you always do," she said, patting Stone's neck. "He'll want to go this morning. He already knows something is up. But hold him in until you turn him at the quarter pole, then let him go in a burst, just as if you were coming out of a starting gate."

Melanie nodded. She could feel Stone's muscles bunched beneath her, and a bubble of nerves rose in her own stomach. What if she lost control? She grimaced and chased away the thought.

"Okay, then." Samantha lifted the stopwatch in her hand. Melanie took it as her cue and headed for the opening to the track. As they jogged counter-clockwise she lifted her face to meet the wind, letting it flow down her neck and over her arms. She reined Stone in when they reached the red and white marker, then turned him toward the wire. He knew what was coming and took off before she even squeezed her knees to signal him. It took her by surprise, and she had to struggle for a moment to regain her position in the saddle. Then she leaned low over his neck, feeding the reins up to him, and felt his power explode beneath her. Stone's legs extended, hammering out a rhythm that stuck in Melanie's head like some primal drumbeat. His black mane whipped in the wind, caressing her face as she guided him down the track—not like a race car careening out of control, but like a guided missile. Speed was their common goal as they flew homeward, not separately, as horse and rider, but as one. Melanie couldn't remember a time when anything had ever felt so right. They whipped under the finish wire, and she saw Ian, Samantha, and Ashleigh in a blur on the sideline, jumping up and down, yelling something she couldn't quite hear as she worked to bring Stone down from his high and end what had felt so perfect.

Stone slowed, gradually dropping his pace down to a canter and then a jog, and finally an extended walk. He was barely blowing as they rounded the track and headed back to where Ian, Samantha, and Ashleigh were waiting at the gate.

"Wow! What a time!" Samantha cried, holding up the stopwatch.

Ashleigh peered at the stopwatch and nodded her agreement. "Stone's best ever!" she exclaimed.

Melanie leaned forward to pat Stone's neck. "Really?" she asked breathlessly.

Ian slapped the rail in a gesture of satisfaction. "Really," he said. "You rode him great, Mel."

The rush of adrenaline left Melanie in a whoosh. Suddenly she felt exhausted but wonderful. She had helped Stone clock his best time ever! She couldn't wait to tell someone. But whom could she tell?

Later that afternoon, Melanie leaned on the top board of a white fence, watching a chestnut horse grazing on the other side of the field and waiting for Kevin. The horse was a deep copper color with an even darker reddish tail and perfect conformation. His name was Pride's Perfection, a full brother to Perfect Heart's unborn foal, and out of the famous Wonder's Pride. Melanie knew that they'd been working with the colt for a few months now, getting him out on the track for a few workouts. He was almost ready to go into full training, and Melanie longed to try him out. She knew the honor would probably go to Naomi, or maybe Ashleigh would do it herself. Still, a girl could dream, and Melanie did as she watched the colt lift his magnificent head, his nostrils flaring. Then he reeled and took off across the grassy field, kicking and bucking as though he were still a yearling.

"He's really going to be something."

Melanie started at the deep voice breaking into her thoughts. "Kevin, what took you so long?" she demanded.

"Mike and I were talking about the yearling sale. He wants me to help train the horses for loading, and go along to the sale," Kevin explained.

"That sounds like fun," Melanie commented.

"Well, it's my job—Mike's paying me, but it will be fun. I'm lucky to have a job that's so much fun," Kevin said. He tugged on a lock of Melanie's hair. "Orange today? What does orange mean?" he asked.

"It means orange was the only flavor of Kool-Aid in the cupboard last night," Melanie answered with a half smile. "Or maybe I just wanted hair close to your color!"

Kevin ran a hand through his unruly auburn hair. "Aw, my hair's more brown than red. But let's make a deal—I won't make fun of your hair if you don't make fun of mine."

"Deal!" Melanie stuck out her hand to shake, and Kevin grasped it firmly.

They turned to watch Perfection in the distance, Kevin propping a foot up on the lower fence board. The colt had settled down to graze. "How's the exercise riding going?" Kevin asked.

Melanie beamed. "It's great!" she exclaimed. "Today

I got to let Stone out in a full gallop. It was fantastic—we went so fast we were tearing up the track. I think he could be a big winner one day. He's much faster than I ever realized." She knew she was rattling on, but she didn't care. Kevin understood. "Sam said it was Stone's best time ever."

"Is that a good thing?" Kevin asked with a wry smile.

Melanie knew he was joking but she answered anyway, punching him on the arm. "Of course it's good, you idiot!" She stopped and gazed out at Perfection again. "Can you believe I'm actually learning to be an exercise rider?" she asked dreamily. *Maybe I really will get to ride Perfection one day*, she thought.

"Sounds to me like you already are one," Kevin commented.

"I guess I am, but I'm still in training. I learn something new every day. It's like a dream come true."

Kevin took his foot down from the rail. "You know, Mike says he's going to let me breeze some horses after the yearling sale."

"He is?" Melanie grabbed his hand. "That's great!"

"I guess," Kevin agreed, smiling. "Let's go see Perfect Heart," he suggested. "Mike says it looks like her milk bag is starting to fill up. Maybe she'll have that foal this week."

"You read my mind," Melanie said as she walked beside Kevin toward the broodmare barn. "What do you think the foal will be, filly or colt?"

41

Kevin shrugged, then seemed to decide to play the game. "Colt. Boys are better," he said, grinning.

"Are not!" Melanie shouted, and punched him again. "What color do you think it will be?" she demanded.

"That one's easy. Chestnut, of course," Kevin responded. "Pride and Heart are chestnuts."

"Yeah, I guess that one *was* easy. Any markings?" Melanie asked, her eyes dancing.

"None. He'll be plain old chestnut. But plain can be beautiful, too," Kevin reminded her.

"Plain can be beautiful," Melanie agreed, "but I think it'll have a heart on its forehead, just like its dam."

Kevin grabbed her hand and started to run, pulling her behind him. "We'll see soon enough."

Melanie laughed, and they ran together all the way to the broodmare barn. She glanced over at Kevin as they walked down the aisle and noticed that all of a sudden he looked very serious. "Kev, what's wrong?" she asked.

"Well, it's just that I've kind of missed you the past week or so. Everyone has."

Melanie let go of his hand and stood still.

"I know you like what you're doing," Kevin continued, "but you have to take a break sometime. You exercise in the morning, do stable work after school, and then work on your homework all night. Don't you ever have fun anymore?"

Melanie gulped. "You know how busy I am," she answered defensively. "I'm not taking lessons at Mona's right now, so I thought I'd see more of you around here."

"But what about the trail ride last Sunday? I know you said you forgot, but did you really?" Kevin demanded.

Melanie frowned. "Of course I just forgot. Don't you think I'd have been there if I remembered?"

"Sure." Kevin's voice was dull. "But why weren't you at Dylan's soccer game last night? I looked everywhere for you. I told Katie I was sure you'd be there. I know you were tired, but you could have come over for a little while if you really wanted to."

Melanie spun around. "Soccer game? What soccer game?" she asked, startled.

It was Kevin's turn to look bewildered. "You mean you didn't know? It was a special charity game at St. Margaret's," he explained. "Christina didn't tell you?"

Melanie felt her face burn. "No, she did not tell me one thing about it. Was she supposed to?" she asked.

"Yeah," Kevin said uneasily. "Everyone wondered where you were."

"And what did Christina say?"

Kevin's brow wrinkled. "She just said you were working here at Whitebrook," he said.

Suddenly Melanie felt numb. Her legs were weak and her heart was racing.

"We're meeting for another trail ride tomorrow

night. Did she tell you about that?" Kevin asked.

"No!" Melanie shook her head sadly. A part of her was getting angry. She swallowed hard to make the anger go away. She and Christina were friends, but . . . Christina wouldn't exclude her on purpose and let their friends think it was Melanie's choice. Would she?

4

MELANIE HAD ALL AFTERNOON TO LET ANGER EAT AT HER. That evening she stormed into Christina's room, where her cousin was poring over homework at her desk.

"Why didn't you tell me about Dylan's soccer game?" Melanie demanded. She knew she was probably blowing things way out of proportion, but she was so angry she practically spit out the words.

"I forgot," Christina said, shrugging. "If you can forget things, so can I. And who invited you into my room?"

"I didn't know I needed an invitation," Melanie replied. "I thought you were my friend! Why are you acting like this? What did I do that's so bad?" she demanded.

"Oh, you need a list?" Christina snapped. "How about when I visited you in New York and you tried to make me look bad by putting me on the worst horse there?"

"Give me a break!" Melanie exclaimed. "That was so long ago!" She put her hands on her hips, glaring at Christina. "And this fight isn't about what happened in New York, it's about you leaving me out on purpose," she added.

"I told you, I forgot," Christina repeated, but the excuse sounded lame.

"If you just forgot, then why didn't you tell everyone that instead of making them think I ditched them?" Melanie asked.

Christina shrugged, and Melanie's anger swelled. "You remembered to go, so you should have remembered to tell me, too," she said. "And what about the trail ride tomorrow night? Were you ever planning on telling me about that?" she demanded.

"I was going to tell you tonight—before you barged in here uninvited and attacked me!" Christina's face was flushed, and she looked like she was going to cry. A flash of guilt made Melanie think twice. Maybe Christina really had forgotten.

"I didn't attack you. I just wanted to know why you didn't tell me about the soccer game," Melanie explained.

Christina's voice was angry when she answered. "I'm not your message service, Melanie. Get out of my room. *Now,* please."

"Fine!" Melanie slammed the door so hard on her

46

way out she thought Ashleigh might hear and come to ask what was going on. But she didn't, and Melanie went to her own bedroom.

Melanie lay on her bed and thought about all the fun times she and Christina had had together. They had been best friends for the past year. They'd hardly ever disagreed, and except for one occasion at riding camp that summer, they'd pretty much always stood up for each other. So what had made Christina suddenly act so cold and distant? Melanie stared at the ceiling for a long time before she fell asleep, wondering how the whole mess had ever started.

On Sunday morning Melanie ran the brush over Trib's neck one last time. The brown and white pinto pony was roly-poly fat, and acting even more ornery than usual, pawing to upset the bucket of grooming tools that sat by Melanie's feet. Hoof picks, brushes, and combs scattered.

"Oh, Trib," Melanie sighed, and stopped to right the bucket, scooping the brushes and hoof picks back inside, and moving the bucket out of the pony's reach. Usually she was more patient with Trib, but worrying about Christina and how she would act on the trail ride that day kept her mind too occupied to fit patience in. They'd barely spoken for the past week. Christina was avoiding her and had even made a point of getting to the bus stop last every morning so they didn't have time to talk before sitting separately on the crowded bus. And except for Kevin, she wasn't sure how their usual gang of riding friends felt, either. Dylan, Cassidy, and Katie probably all thought she was snubbing them. They waved when they passed each other in the halls, and they saw each other at lunch, but she hadn't seen them outside of school since she'd started riding on the track.

Melanie sighed again. Then she took a deep breath. She grabbed hold of Trib's halter and looked the pony in the eye. "You be good for me today," she said. "I have enough to worry about without you dumping me in front of everyone."

Trib tossed his head, and Melanie had to laugh. "No one can get through to that ornery brain of yours, can they?" She couldn't help but love the pony. Trib had been Christina's show pony until she'd outgrown him and Aunt Ashleigh and Uncle Mike had purchased Sterling Dream off the track for her. But Melanie was short enough to ride the pony and she had done a lot of that, taking lessons from Mona Gardener with him and showing in events at camp. She'd even taken Trib with her to New York when her dad wanted her to move back home after he'd gotten married. But Trib had hated being pent up in the city stables with nowhere to be turned out and had become terribly depressed. It was as if Trib had read her mind—that was exactly how Melanie had felt there, too. Finally her dad had realized what was wrong and sent them both back to live at Whitebrook. She loved her dad and missed him, but her heart was in the country, at Whitebrook.

"Trib, you and I have been through a lot together." Melanie hugged the pony, and Trib surprised her by standing still for it. A few minutes later she had the pony saddled and bridled and was leading him from the barn to meet the others at Mona's.

The sun was low in the sky, and although the air was cool, the sunlight felt warm on Melanie's face. The group of friends was to meet at four o'clock for an hour-long ride along the woodland trails that bordered Whitebrook and the fields surrounding Mona's farm. Melanie knew Christina was already there. She'd left early on Sterling. Melanie mounted and turned Trib toward Mona's at a brisk trot, pulling up when she heard the sound of hoofbeats coming up behind her. She laughed when she heard Kevin yell—his voice came out all bouncy and full of trot. "M-e-el, w-a-ait for me-e-e!" he cried.

She stopped Trib and waited for Kevin to catch up. His horse, Jasper, was a red sorrel Anglo-Arab gelding with a cream-colored mane and tail. Jasper had the arched neck carriage of an Arab, with the deep shoulders and elegant head of a Thoroughbred. Melanie smiled. Kevin always made her feel better. Just knowing that he wanted to ride with her over to Mona's meant a lot, especially now, when it seemed like all Melanie's friends were mad at her.

Kevin slowed Jasper to a walk, and they turned the horses together, moving through the grassy pasture in unison.

"Thanks for coming with me," Melanie said gratefully.

Kevin bowed at the waist, a grin on his face. "But of course, madam!" he said dramatically, and Melanie laughed.

The grass waved in the breeze as they passed through it. Jasper's stride was long and fluid, and Trib jogged along at his side to keep up, his short legs pumping through the thick goldenrod and dark crabgrass. Tall foxtails, their brown heads bent with the breeze, dotted the autumn-brown meadow.

"Does everyone know I'm coming?" Melanie asked, fighting away the lump rising in her throat. "Do you think they really want me there?"

"Is that why you have those blue streaks in your hair today?" Kevin asked thoughtfully as he looked down at Melanie. "Are you really worried about what everyone will think?"

Melanie pushed at a strand of hair clinging to the sweat that had gathered at the edge of her riding helmet. "Yeah," she admitted, ignoring the hair question. "I am nervous. According to Christina, everyone thinks I've dumped them or something."

Kevin laughed. "They don't think that!" he insisted.

Melanie bit her lip, a little perturbed. Maybe it was just nerves, but she didn't like being laughed at.

"Okay, if you're so smart, you tell me what they do think. I didn't show up for the first trail ride because I forgot, and I didn't go to Dylan's soccer game because I didn't know about it, and Christina keeps telling everybody it's because I'm too busy." Her words came out in a rush, and she allowed herself to get angry because it kept the tears at bay.

"Aw, Mel." Kevin's voice was low and soft. "They just think that you and Christina are like sisters, and sisters fight. I guarantee you they don't even think it's about them. It's between you and Christina."

Melanie turned Trib down a worn path to the left. She could see the barn at Gardener Farm just ahead. The pony moved down the narrow path, with Jasper just behind. Melanie watched Trib's brown ears bob as he stepped eagerly forward, the proud leader, and then she glanced over her shoulder to smile at Kevin.

They rode in silence for a while. As they came over the rise Melanie could see the others leaning against the board fence that surrounded the riding ring, each holding their mount by a lead shank. Mona was there in jeans and chaps, a baseball cap pulled low over her short brown hair. At first the others didn't see Kevin and Melanie ride up, but Melanie could hear Mona giving them last-minute details on an upcoming event. Then Katie heard them approaching and shouted hello, and soon everyone was turning and waving.

"Well, the lost sheep finally came home!" Mona said. "Where have you been?"

Melanie blushed. "I've been training with Ashleigh and Samantha at Whitebrook."

"We heard," Katie interrupted. "To be an exercise rider! That's so exciting!"

"Yeah," Cassidy joined in. "How do you like it?"

"Have you breezed any horses yet?" Dylan added. "Or are they still making you watch from the sidelines?"

Melanie started to laugh. "Wait! One question at a time," she said. "Yes, I love it. And yes, I'm breezing Heart of Stone every day, and it's the best!"

"Well, don't forget everything you learned over here," Mona said. "A little common sense goes a long way when you're riding racehorses."

Melanie nodded respectfully. She knew Mona was right. She'd learned so much from Mona's lessons, things she used every time she got up on Stone. Melanie remembered how Mona had made her stop trying to boss Trib around and become the pony's partner instead. Melanie had discovered that working together with her mount worked best no matter what kind of horse she was riding.

"You kids get out on the trail before it gets too late." Mona waved at them as she crossed the ring, all business now.

As the others mounted their horses, Melanie glanced around, wondering where Christina was. Then she spotted her sitting on Sterling, standing still under a maple tree. She must have left the group when she saw Melanie coming. When she realized Melanie was looking at her, she looked away.

Cassidy was on her gorgeous Canadian warmblood jumper, Rebound. Cassidy rode two show horses, and for a while it had looked as though she might have to sell both of them because of financial problems in her family, but so far they were holding their own, and Cassidy had been able to keep both Rebound and her Thoroughbred hunter, Welly. Every time Melanie saw Cassidy she crossed her fingers and said a prayer that things would work out for the family.

Katie was on her bay pony, Seabreeze, and Dylan was riding his chestnut, Dakota. As they fell into line, moving across the field toward Tall Oak Trail, Melanie thought the day would have been just perfect if only Christina would act like her friend again and talk to her.

After they'd gone down the hill and hit the part of the trail that widened and wound through the majestic oaks, they spread out so they could ride side by side and talk. Crisp, colored leaves waved above them, making crackling sounds in the breeze. But as they moved deeper into the wooded area, the breeze stopped and the air felt warmer.

"So tell us what it's like," Cassidy asked, her blond hair sticking out like wings from the sides of her riding helmet. "What's it like to gallop like crazy on a real racetrack?" She looked at Melanie, eyebrows raised.

"It's indescribable," Melanie answered, and then

proceeded to describe the indescribable. "Heart of Stone's so fast," she said. "Faster than any horse I've ever ridden. When his hooves are pounding on the track, I can feel it through my whole body."

"Faster than Trib?" Dylan asked. "Hey, remember that time the bee stung Trib when he was in the ring and he dumped you?" Dylan let out a roaring laugh, and everyone else joined in. "I'm sorry," he said, gasping between words. "It wasn't really funny. But if you could have seen yourself!"

Cassidy chuckled, and Katie joined in. "You have to admit it was funny, Mel," Katie said. "Trib was crow-hopping across the ring, and you looked like a cowboy riding a bucking bronco!"

Melanie grinned in spite of herself. "I know, I know. I just have one question—what do you guys do when I'm not around to laugh at?" she asked.

Cassidy swatted a fly off Rebound's neck. "It's just not as much fun," she said seriously.

"I can hardly believe we still have three days until we have to go back to school," Dylan commented, glancing at Christina, who was being so obviously, stubbornly silent.

"I know, it's so great," Katie said. "Is anyone going into town for the Fall Fest?"

"I am," Cassidy said. She wrinkled her nose. "My mom signed us both up to help with the school's lollipop booth. She wants us to do more together."

"I wasn't planning to," Dylan said, "but maybe I'll

try to come in." He grinned. "Just so I can buy a lolli-pop from you!"

Melanie shrugged. "I'm going to be busy with Pirate and exercise riding," she said.

Christina kept quiet, holding Sterling back to tail the group. Melanie couldn't stand her cousin's stubborn silence any longer. She dropped back to ride beside Sterling, hoping to bring Christina into the conversation. Melanie didn't feel angry anymore; she only wanted to smooth things over.

But Christina moved Sterling up the trail, away from Melanie, riding alongside the others. "Are you guys ready for the schooling show at McDonough next week?" she asked. A moment later the group was engaged in a deep conversation about which judges would be there and how high the course would be. Melanie knew they weren't excluding her on purpose, but it felt funny not to be a part of that anymore.

Finally Kevin dropped back to ride beside Melanie and she glanced at him, unable to keep the hurt look out of her eyes. Kevin ran a hand through his wavy auburn hair and shrugged. Then he grinned and yelled out, "Race you guys!" And before Melanie knew what was happening he'd taken off, leaving her and the others laughing in the dust.

On Monday morning the alarm clock let out a shrill ring at 4 A.M. Melanie's first instinct was to turn it off,

55

roll over, and go back to sleep. But she couldn't do that. She knew Ashleigh and Samantha were probably up, maybe even already in the barn. So she hurried down the stairs, grabbed some toast and juice, and headed for the stables, her desire to sleep late gone, excitement setting in. The lights from the barn glowed in the dusky morning.

Samantha and Ashleigh were there, and so was Naomi. The three women had two horses in crossties in the wide aisle. Melanie recognized Stone right away, but it took her a moment to figure out who the second horse was—a bright, coppery chestnut. As she drew closer she saw the white blaze that ran down his face and thought at first it was Pride. But Melanie quickly realized her mistake when the horse tossed its head and danced sideways in the aisle as Ashleigh slipped a light racing saddle down over its back. It was Pride's colt, Pride's Perfection. Just down the aisle Naomi was tacking up Stone with her own saddle.

"Hey, what's going on?" Melanie asked, puzzled.

"We're going to start you on Perfection," Ashleigh answered, watching Melanie's face for a reaction.

"Me?" Melanie was surprised. "On Perfection?"

"That's right," Samantha said as she lifted Stone's front hoof to pick it out. "With the long weekend you have off school, we thought you'd have some extra time to spend with Perfection and get to know him."

"But what about Stone?" Melanie asked, surprised by the sudden change in plans.

"Naomi's breezing him today." Samantha straightened from picking Stone's hooves. "Is that okay with you?"

"Sure!" Melanie exclaimed, her excitement bubbling to the surface.

Naomi ran a brush over Stone's dusty back. "It's about time I finally got to ride Stone again," she said mischievously.

"Oh, did I take him from you?" Melanie asked.

"Nope," Naomi said. "Just thought I'd get your goat."

"And today we're going to start from the gate," Ashleigh said, referring to the starting gate on the track.

"Cool!" Melanie cried. She tucked her riding helmet under her arm and took Perfection's reins. This was getting better and better. Naomi took Stone's reins, and together they walked toward the track, leading their mounts. Melanie glanced over at Stone. Like a gentle giant, the dark bay loomed over Naomi's head with a placid expression. Melanie sighed. She had grown attached to the big horse, but she knew part of her training was learning to ride all sorts of horses. Besides, she wouldn't miss a chance to ride Perfection for the world!

Ashleigh and Samantha fell behind them, talking as they walked, and Melanie strained her ears and tried to hear what was being said over the clatter of hoofbeats on the gravel path.

"I'm so glad Melanie is following through on this," Ashleigh was saying. "I didn't want to push her the way I did Christina."

"What do you mean?" Samantha asked. "You're not pushy, Ash."

"With Christina I was. I let her know how much I wanted her to like racing. But she likes to jump. I should have just accepted it from the start."

"Oh, don't be so hard on yourself," Samantha said.

Melanie bit her lip. If what Ashleigh said was true, it was no wonder Christina was mad at her—in a way, Melanie was replacing Christina! But Melanie's anger at her cousin nudged any sympathetic thoughts out of her mind and she shrugged them away, not wanting to care.

As they drew closer to the training track Melanie saw Ian McLean hunched over the rail, blowing on his hands in the cool morning air.

"Big day, huh, Melanie?" he asked, squinting in the sunlight.

Melanie grinned nervously and reached forward to straighten Perfection's mane.

"She can handle him," Naomi said encouragingly. "So, boss, what are we doing today?" she added.

Ian took hold of Stone's bridle, and Naomi leaned over to listen to his instructions. Ashleigh and Samantha stood on either side of Perfection's head, and Melanie furrowed her brow in concentration.

"Okay, Melanie," Ashleigh said. "This guy's been

loaded into the gate a time or two, but he's still green at breaking."

Samantha looked at Melanie. "Do you remember watching us work with him in the gate in the spring?"

Melanie nodded. She remembered. At first Pride's Perfection had been terrified of the gate and wanted nothing to do with it. Naomi had walked him into the open gate the first time, and they left both the front and back open, so the young horse could escape if he wanted to. But Pride still fought, rearing up, pawing the air, his eyes rolling in terror. Melanie had sat on the hill and watched them talk him through it. When they finally closed the back gate, the colt backed hard against it, his rump pressing his tail flat, cowering and too scared to move, until he realized he could shoot straight out the front. Again and again they repeated the exercise until at last he'd relaxed and stayed put. Finally they shut the front, too, and it had started all over again—the pawing, the snorting, the whinnies of frustration. Melanie couldn't remember when he'd decided not to be afraid, but it had taken all afternoon to get him used to standing inside.

"Well, now we have another problem," Samantha explained, smiling wryly. "He's too comfortable in the gate!"

Melanie shot Samantha a questioning look, and she continued. "When the gate flies open, he just strolls out, without a care in the world."

Melanie laughed. "So how can I change that?"

Ashleigh glanced at Ian and Naomi. "Naomi and Stone are going to load in next to you. When Stone breaks from the gate—and he will—we hope it will influence Perfection to do the same. I've seen it happen many times, a young horse watching an older one and learning just what to do."

Naomi smiled. "This guy is the opposite of Perfection," she said as she patted Stone's thick neck. "He gets really worked up in the starting gate. He knows what's about to happen—that he'll explode out of there and run like crazy—and he has trouble containing himself. Sometimes he uses everything he has in the start. It's a fun ride, but it's not so great for winning races."

"Naomi!" Ashleigh scolded, her eyes sparkling. "Bad horses are not fun." She turned back to Melanie. "We're counting on that competitive streak in Perfection to surface. If it does, you may just have the ride of your life, Mel."

Melanie's body was rigid with nervous anticipation. She took a deep breath. What would happen when they broke from the gate? Would Perfection challenge Stone and try to take the lead, or would he just saunter out leisurely? Either way, Melanie would have to hold on tight!

As they neared the gate Stone began to prance and jig. Sensing the older horse's excitement, Perfection threw his head and began to sidestep. But it was all just for show, and both of them loaded quietly. The slam of metal as Ian shut the loading door sent a shiver down Melanie's spine. It was her first time inside the gate, and never before had she felt so terrified and so thrilled. She glanced at Naomi, but the older girl was crouched low, her face hidden. There was a creak of metal, followed by an eerie silence. Perfection pawed the ground and snorted restlessly. Melanie checked her reins and crouched down, looking dead ahead between the chestnut colt's ears. She heard Stone snort, and all at once the buzzer sounded and the gate flew wide open.

Melanie thought she had prepared herself, but she was not ready for the burst of energy that exploded underneath her. Perfection shot out of the gate, just seconds behind Stone. Then, before she could stop it from happening, the colt had the bit in his teeth and he lunged ahead, passing Stone in a blur.

Melanie felt the earth whizzing past, and tried to focus on the track ahead. She heard Mona's voice in her head. *Pulley rein . . . use a pulley rein to slow him.* That's what Mona had always told Melanie to do when Trib rushed the jumps on the cross-country course, and it worked every time. She tried it now, pulling up on her inside rein in steady half-halts and gaining control of the bit again. Soon Perfection had settled into a manageable gallop.

Melanie concentrated hard on the bundle of energy she was riding, trying to locate the source of his excitement, to make contact with his mind. As she did she realized Perfection was slowing down of his own accord, mimicking the older horse, who had fallen in behind him. At first Stone's excitement had fired the young horse up—when Stone leaped from the gate, Perfection had followed suit. Now the older horse was back in control and Naomi was keeping him to a sensible gallop. Melanie kept her hands light and sat back to signal the colt to slow even more. Perfection responded by dropping back to join Stone, and they ran neck and neck, passing under the finish line in unison.

Melanie felt exhilaration building inside her, just as it had when Stone had gone all out for her. But this time it was an even better feeling. She was the first to get the two-year-old to run from the gate. More important, she had used her wits to make Perfection do what he was supposed to do. Instead of fighting with him and letting the fear that he would run away with her take over, Melanie had succeeded in listening to the colt and worked with him. It was a fantastic feeling.

Naomi was slowing Stone beside her. Gradually both horses dropped to a trot, then a swinging walk. Melanie grinned at Naomi, who was smiling.

"It worked!" Naomi said. "Perfection followed Stone's instruction and did what he thought he was supposed to do."

Melanie nodded.

Naomi patted Stone's neck. "You're a good boy," she said. "We ought to call you the Professor."

Melanie looked at Stone and laughed. With his head bobbing and his eyes dead ahead, he did look kind of dignified, the way a professor should look.

"Nice," Ian said, "very nice."

"Good run, girls," Ashleigh added as they drew closer. "Our strategy worked." Her eyes showed her satisfaction. "You handled that very well, Melanie," she said. "Very well."

Samantha nodded in agreement.

Melanie beamed, basking in their praise. *Now I know why I love this so much*, Melanie thought. *It's the first thing I've ever been really good at.*

That evening Melanie sat down next to Christina at the dining room table.

Christina had schoolwork spread out on the dark tabletop and was coloring in graphs with markers.

"How was your lesson today?" Melanie asked. She knew Christina had started lessons at Samantha's three afternoons a week. They still weren't talking, and Melanie wondered if Christina would even answer.

"Fine," Christina answered as she flipped through the pages of her book, her finger tracing a passage as she read. Then she went back to filling in graph lines with a purple marker.

Melanie tried again. "Is it lonely at Samantha's without the rest of the gang?" she asked.

"No, it's fine. Parker's there, and sometimes Kevin,

when he stops by to see his sister," Christina said.

"How is Parker these days?"

Christina put down her marker and looked up. "He's fine," she said quietly, and sighed. "Melanie, look. I only have tonight and two more days to finish this, and it's the final project for this unit," she explained.

Christina sounded annoyed, and Melanie couldn't help but feel hurt. "Oh, okay," Melanie said, and turned away, wondering how to fix their broken friendship. Just then the phone rang on the table beside her and she picked up the receiver, keeping her back to Christina. It was her father.

"Hi, pumpkin."

"Dad! How was your trip?" she exclaimed happily.

"It was just fine. Same old thing—you know, crowds mobbing the band, people clawing to meet the next big rock star, and me, your old dad, right in the middle of it all," he said with a laugh.

"Just where you like to be," Melanie said, her heart warming to hear her father's voice.

Her dad chuckled. "I guess you're right. So what have you been up to lately?" he asked.

"Dad, you won't believe what I've been doing! It's so exciting. Samantha and Ashleigh have been training me to become an exercise rider on the track here at Whitebrook. I got to ride a two-year-old today. His name is Pride's Perfection, and he was great! When he shot out of that gate I felt like I was in heaven."

"Whoa, whoa there. You've been riding race-horses?" her father demanded. "We're talking Thoroughbreds? And you're jockeying?"

Melanie hesitated, her mind registering a warning. "Yes," she answered warily.

"That sounds awfully risky, hon," her father said seriously. "Let me talk to Ashleigh."

Melanie's mind scrambled. Ashleigh was in the barn. She couldn't call her, and something told her not to even suggest it. Not now. "Ashleigh's not here," she said. "Why do you want to talk to her?"

"I'd just like to hear her thoughts on this. Letting you ride that blind horse is scary enough, but race-horses . . . that's another thing altogether," her father cautioned.

"Pirate? You're worried about Pirate? He's the safest horse I've ever ridden. Even safer than Trib," Melanie insisted.

"Trib is a little pony, not a horse, and frankly, Melanie, when it comes to horses, you don't always think with a clear head," her father warned.

Melanie's face burned. She was getting angry and she couldn't stop herself. "I love horses more than anything, Dad," she said tersely. "And I know what I am doing. This is my absolute dream. Please don't take it away! This is what I want to do for the rest of my life!"

There was a long sigh at the other end of the line. "Melanie, have your aunt call me," her father insisted. "And until I talk to her, I forbid you to ride any more of those dangerous half-trained animals," he added.

"You can't forbid me!" Melanie was shouting now. "You don't know anything about them. You don't know anything about horses!"

"Melanie." Her dad took a deep breath, as though he were weighing his words. "Do you remember what happened to Milky Way?" he asked gently.

Melanie felt a wave of nausea. How could her dad bring that up? She groaned. Would she ever get past what had happened with Milky Way? It was true. She *had* caused her favorite horse's death in New York. But she'd been a mixed-up, unhappy kid back then, too quick to take chances. Even so, it had been a terrible, terrible accident—it hadn't been her fault.

There was silence on the other end of the line. Melanie swallowed the lump that rose in her throat. Her thoughts were racing, trying to build a defense, but when her dad spoke again, he seemed to be finished.

"Just have your aunt call me," he said again, his voice soft. "Maybe we can work something out," he added.

As Melanie turned to hang up, she caught Christina's gaze. Her cousin was studying her intently—she had heard every word.

5

MELANIE SLAMMED THE PHONE RECEIVER ONTO ITS HOOK. "He can't stop me from riding!" she stormed.

Christina put the cap on her pen, her brow furrowing. "Your dad doesn't want you to exercise-ride?" she asked.

"No!" Melanie jumped up and began to pace. She stubbed her toe on her book bag, which she had thrown on the floor earlier in the day. The pain in her toe only made her angrier. She kicked the book bag, hard. "He says I'll get hurt! He doesn't know one thing about horses, but he thinks he can tell me what to do! It's just not fair!" she exclaimed.

Christina smoothed her paper and picked up a green marker. "He *is* your dad," she said slowly.

"I know," Melanie said, still pacing. "But that doesn't make it fair. Why do people always say that kind of thing? 'He's your dad' or 'You have to respect him.' I know all that! But what about me?" Melanie demanded. She sat down at the table and put her face in her hands. She felt close to tears. "He wants to talk to Ashleigh," she mumbled through her hands. "He told me to tell her to call him."

Christina chewed the end of her marker. "So tell her," she said.

Melanie could feel her cousin studying her. She thought a moment before she answered.

"No," she said. "I can't. I mean, what if Dad tells her not to let me ride? Don't say anything yet, Chris," she pleaded. "Please—I just need a few days. Give me a chance to work something out."

But Christina didn't promise Melanie anything. She just shrugged and went back to her homework, ending the discussion. Melanie had to hope her cousin would keep her mouth shut.

That night Melanie rolled over on her side and replayed the conversation with her father in her head. *Maybe we can work something out,* her dad had said. What was that supposed to mean? She rolled again, now lying face up. She traced one long crack in the ceiling with her eyes. As the tears welled up, the crack began to blur. How could he do this to her—ruin her life like this just when everything was going so well?

She got up and padded down the hall to Christina's

room. The floor felt cold beneath her toes. She peeked into the bedroom. "Chris, are you still awake?" she whispered loudly.

"Yes." Christina's voice was muffled.

"Can we talk?" Melanie called.

"I guess," Christina said, and sat up, curling her legs to make room for Melanie to sit at the bottom of the bed. "Are you still upset about your dad?" Christina asked.

"Yeah." Melanie ran a hand through her hair. "What am I going to do?"

Christina shrugged. She didn't look at Melanie. "I don't know. I guess you should listen to him. Anyway, you can always start taking lessons again. You were just starting to get good at jumping and dressage."

"But I'm much better on the track," Melanie answered miserably. "I've come too far to quit. And I'm finally good at something."

"Oh, Mel, you're good at lots of things." Christina sighed. "Did you tell Mom to call your dad?"

Melanie fidgeted. "Not yet. I'm trying to figure out some kind of defense first. I have to keep exercise-riding," she said.

"Stop saying that! You don't *have* to exercise-ride," Christina interrupted, sounding angry. "I don't understand you, Melanie. How did you get so obsessed with this thing? You're just like my mom—no time for anything but racing. And she loves that you are so into it, too." Christina threw the blankets off her legs and pulled her knees up to her chin. She eyed her cousin coolly. "If you don't tell my mom what your dad said, I will!" she threatened.

Now Melanie felt her anger welling up. "You wouldn't do that!" she declared.

"I will," Christina insisted.

"You're just jealous because your mom likes that I want to race. She's spending lots of time with me and maybe you don't like it!" Melanie shouted. She ran her hand through her hair furiously. "But being a tattletale won't make things better," she added.

Christina stared at the tops of her knees. "You're wrong," she said. "I'm not jealous. I never wanted to exercise-ride. I like eventing. Why doesn't anyone in this house understand that? I want to ride in the Olympics. Racing is just plain boring."

"Well, good for you!" Melanie said sarcastically, as she got up from the bed. "Thanks for being so supportive." She turned on her heel and walked out of the room.

Back in bed, Melanie still couldn't sleep. This latest fight with Christina had just made things worse. She'd thought her cousin would understand and help her figure out what to do about her father and Ashleigh. After all, it was Christina who had saved Melanie from having to stay in the city. She'd helped convince Melanie's dad to let her come live at Whitebrook when he had been determined to keep her in New York with him.

Melanie rolled over and buried her face in her pillow. Ever since she'd moved in with the Reeses, Christina had been there for her. They'd both been so excited, and Christina had even said that having Melanie there was just like having a sister. So what was going on? Maybe Christina was starting to resent Melanie's presence. Then Melanie remembered what she had heard Ashleigh tell Samantha about pushing Christina to ride on the track, and it hit her: *Christina must feel like I'm trying to take her place.*

The barn lights gave off a warm glow in the darkness of early morning as Melanie walked down the path. The air was cool and she shivered. In a few minutes she would see Ashleigh in the barn. She knew she should tell her about her father's phone call, but she couldn't. Not until she had galloped Pride's Perfection one more time.

"This guy's raring to go," Ashleigh said when she saw Melanie, patting Perfection's bright chestnut neck as she spoke. The colt was in crossties, standing in the center aisle. He pawed the floor and rolled his eyes.

"Am I late?" Melanie asked, surprised.

Ashleigh consulted her watch. "Nope. Right on time. I guess I was early today," she explained. "Ready for another great workout?" she asked eagerly.

Perfection half reared, pulling the crossties tight and coming back down again, his shoes ringing on the cement.

71

Melanie eyed him warily. "What's with him today?" she asked.

"I think he's just feeling his oats. It's this cooler fall weather. It gets them all fired up," Ashleigh explained. "Anyway, let's get going—I already groomed him for you," she added.

Melanie took Perfection's saddle from the rack and began to tack the colt up. The barn was quiet, and Melanie felt awkward in the knowledge that she was keeping something from her aunt.

"Where's Sam?" she asked.

"She'll be here soon. Her stud has been acting up, and she thought working him early, before everyone arrives for their lessons, might do him some good. She said she'd meet us at the track," Ashleigh told her.

"And what about Ian?" Melanie asked as she fastened the bridle.

"He and Mike and Kev are working with the yearlings today," Ashleigh said. She handed Melanie her helmet. "Ready?" she asked.

Perfection started to paw the aisle again. As soon as Ashleigh started down the aisle with him, he went up on his hind legs.

Melanie's eyes widened. "Boy, he's wound up today!" she exclaimed, suddenly a little frightened. Her father was right—horses could be dangerous. But Melanie was determined, and she pushed his words from her mind.

Ashleigh looked her in the eye. "Do you feel up to dealing with him?" she asked.

"Yes," Melanie said confidently, and rubbed Perfection's shoulder. "We'll be all right, won't we, boy?"

The walk to the track seemed shorter than usual. Ashleigh held tight to Perfection's bridle as he pranced along beside them. "We're going to run Faith in a maiden race at Keeneland tomorrow. Do you want to go?" she asked.

"Sure!" Melanie had always loved the track—the air was always charged with excitement, and every race was a thrill. And now that she was exercise-riding, she could really learn from watching races. "Who's riding?" she asked.

"Naomi," Ashleigh said, grinning.

"Naomi?" Melanie asked, surprised. "But she's never ridden in a race before, has she?"

"Nope," Ashleigh said, her dark eyes dancing. "So I guess it's a maiden race for her, too. She got her jockey's license a little while ago, but this will be her first time in a real race. Ian and I think she knows Faith better than anyone else we could get to ride, and she's ready. I can't wait—she's going to do great."

As promised, Samantha was waiting by the rail. "Starting gate today?" she asked Ashleigh, and Ashleigh nodded.

Melanie remembered her last ride. "Will he go in without Stone?" she asked, suddenly wary.

Ashleigh smiled reassuringly. "We'll find out!" she

73

said. "How did Finn go this morning?" she asked Samantha.

"Really well," Samantha answered. "Every time I work him I love him more. And I hope his foals are all just like him!"

"He's a great foundation for your farm," Ashleigh agreed. "Soon you're going to have a whole barnful of top event horses, and I won't have you around to help me anymore."

Samantha smiled. "Well, I've still got time now," she said. "And I don't want to miss Mel's solo debut!"

Melanie smiled and fastened the chin strap on her helmet.

"How's Christina coming along?" Ashleigh asked as they led Perfection toward the gate.

"She's a promising rider, Ash. I think she can do it all, if she just learns to take her time," Samantha said.

Ashleigh nodded. "Well, I'm just glad Mel decided she liked the track better than eventing." She put her arm over Melanie's shoulder. "She's coming along nicely, too. She's learning faster than I ever expected," she said, giving Melanie a squeeze.

Melanie was still beaming when Samantha gave her a leg up. Perfection balked at the starting gate, then dropped a shoulder so that Melanie almost spilled from the saddle. She pulled him up short, letting him know she was in control. She could feel the animal's muscles bunched under her, and she tightened her grip on the reins. She knew he might feel her tension and feed off it, so she took a deep breath and tried to relax.

"Let him out today," Ashleigh said. "Don't start pulling him in until you pass the second quarter pole. Let's see how fast he gets out of that starting gate without Stone here to help."

Melanie nodded. Perfection braced his legs, pawing at the dirt in front of the gate. Melanie squeezed her knees and Ashleigh pulled at the reins, but he refused to go in. Then, only a moment later, the colt lifted his head and walked into the gate, as if he'd simply decided to do it.

As she waited for the buzzer to sound and the gate to open, every nerve in Melanie's body was on alert. She knew she was going to have her hands full.

"Let's show them you can do it without Stone," she whispered to Perfection. The way he was dancing beneath her told her he would do just that.

Perfection was out of the starting gate before the sound of the buzzer had registered in Melanie's head. Even without Stone, he burst from the gate like a cannonball. Right away she knew it was too much, too fast. Ashleigh had said to let him run, but not like this! The bit was between the colt's teeth, and he had full control. Melanie put all her muscle into the rein, struggling to pull him in. But Perfection wouldn't give up the bit. The rushing wind burned her face and made her eyes tear. Melanie wrestled with her options as Perfection ate up the track beneath them. The colt was a bundle of heat and energy, a stick of live dynamite, and something about that charged Melanie. The pace was grueling and the colt was completely out of control, but Melanie thought her best bet was to let him run himself out. She sat back, keeping pressure on the reins, and tried to ride with him.

Eventually Melanie was able to guide Perfection to the inside of the track, gaining a shred of control. The colt began to slow, and soon she had contact with his mouth again and could relax, riding him at an easy ground-eating gallop. In the next instant Perfection took a large stumbling leap. One minute he was up, and the next he was down and rolling, somewhere to the left of her.

Melanie was airborne, and then she landed, skidding in the dirt. Her left elbow and both forearms took the brunt of the slide, her left leg burning as her jeans ripped open. Melanie closed her eyes for a second, blinking away tears. When she opened them she saw Perfection near her, and her heart sank. He was down on his knees, struggling to stand. Melanie rubbed her eyes. For a split second she saw Milky Way, not Perfection, scrambling on the metal grate on a street in New York City. When she looked at Perfection's eyes, rolling in fear, she saw Milky Way's eyes, and she heard the sound of a blaring cab's horn just before her beloved horse was hit.

Melanie forced away the horrid memory. Beside her Perfection tried two more times to get up before finally standing, braced on all fours but shaking. As she looked at him Melanie swiped at her tears. She heard her dad's voice inside her head: *Remember what happened with Milky Way?*

Then Ashleigh was beside Melanie, helping her to her feet. Her arm came around her in a strong hug. "Are you okay?" Ashleigh asked anxiously. "Where do you hurt?"

Melanie was disoriented. She didn't answer. She looked at Perfection. Samantha was on her knees in front of him, feeling his legs.

I should have listened to Dad and Christina, she thought. *I should have told Ashleigh. I'll probably be grounded for life!* Melanie wiped a hand over her face and watched as Perfection lifted his right foreleg in the air, refusing to put weight on it. Melanie turned her head into her aunt's shoulder and sobbed.

Now Perfection is hurt, she thought. *And it's all my fault.*

6

THEY WALKED BACK TO THE BARN TOGETHER, WITH PERFEC-
tion moving slowly, one step at a time. "He may have
bowed a tendon," Ashleigh said, shaking her head
sadly. "That will put him out of commission six
months to a year. If we're lucky," she added.

Melanie walked at her aunt's shoulder, watching
Perfection step lightly on his injured leg. "I'm sorry,"
she said. "I don't know what happened."

"It's not your fault, Mel," Ashleigh said.

"These things happen all the time," Samantha
added gently. "It was just an accident, and there's
nothing any of us could have done to prevent it. It
could've happened out in the paddock just as easily."

"That's right," Ashleigh agreed, and hugged
Melanie as they walked. "Anyone who spends time
with horses sees accidents often. I'm just glad that

you're okay. What would I have told your father if anything had happened to you?"

Melanie felt a flash of miserable guilt, but she remained silent.

They put Pride's Perfection in his stall, and Ashleigh went to call the vet while Samantha helped Melanie clean off her scrapes in the tack room.

"I hate to walk out on you," Samantha said when Ashleigh had returned from the barn office, "but I have to get back to work at home. Let me know how Perfection makes out with the vet."

"I'll call you first thing," Ashleigh promised.

The vet arrived within the hour. He examined Perfection carefully, asking Melanie to describe the accident in detail. She tried to remember everything that had happened. Had he stepped on anything on the track? No. Had he shown any signs of favoring the leg before the fall? No. Had he broken stride early in the run? No.

"He just stumbled and fell," she told the vet. "I didn't know anything was wrong."

"That can happen with a two-year-old," the vet said. "Young horses are like young children. They're not always steady on their feet, and sometimes they fall."

He felt the injured right leg up and down, checking the left leg, too, as if comparing them. Then he stood up.

"I've got good news and bad news," he announced. "The good news is that the tendon is not bowed. I think we're dealing with a pulled muscle here."

"And the bad news?" Ashleigh asked.

"A muscle pull like this can take as long to heal as a bowed tendon—up to six months."

"So it's almost the same?" Melanie asked.

"No," the vet answered. "A pulled muscle is better. Just about all pulled muscles repair themselves in time. We can't say the same about bowed tendons. They're a horse owner's nightmare, second only to fractures. A lot of times the horse is out of commission for good with a bowed tendon." He shook his head. "At least as far as racing is concerned."

Melanie rubbed Perfection's neck. "So he'll be all right?"

The vet smiled. "I think so," he said. "Cool water soaks will relieve the strain," he told Ashleigh. "Hose it daily, and give him rest, with light hand walking once the swelling's gone down. Treat it as you would treat your own leg if you had a pulled muscle."

Melanie rubbed Perfection's neck again, running her hand down over his chest muscles and onto his upper leg. *What am I going to do?* she wondered. *How am I going to tell Ashleigh that I wasn't even supposed to be riding today?*

"I think we'll let you take care of him, Mel," Ashleigh said. "Would you mind doing that? You could hose him down in the afternoons and keep an eye on the swelling and report back to me. Would that be okay with you?"

"Sure," Melanie agreed. She would do anything to help Perfection get better. She only wished the injury had never happened.

Melanie was glad she still had one more day before school started again. In her room she stared at her reflection in the mirror, then touched the angry red mark that ran down her cheek. She winced, turning away from the mirror and pulled down the window shade. She curled up into a ball on her bed and sobbed, blaming herself for everything that had ever gone wrong in her life.

Melanie heard the door slam as Christina came in from her lesson at Samantha's. She was all cried out, but she stayed in her room, too ashamed of her scrapes and cuts to show her face. Melanie just sat on her bed, wishing she could undo everything that had happened.

That afternoon Kevin called.

"Hey, Mel, Dad's letting me have a cookout. Can you and Christina come over about six?" he asked.

"Sure," Melanie said. "Who else is coming?"

"Everyone. I talked to Katie, Dylan, Cassidy, and Parker. They all said they'd come. Katie's bringing marshmallows for the bonfire."

"A bonfire—that's cool. I'll tell Christina." She adjusted herself on her chair. Her leg was stiff, and her face and arms had long red scrapes on them. She was wearing loose-fitting pajama bottoms and an over-sized T-shirt. She knew that putting on a pair of jeans for the cookout was going to hurt, but she didn't care. "What can we bring?"

"Yourselves!" Kevin said with a laugh. She could almost see Kevin's grin on the other end of the line, and it made her feel a little bit better.

"Maybe we'll bring some hot dogs," Melanie suggested.

"Dad already has hot dogs and hamburgers and rolls." Kevin paused. "But you could bring along some sticks to roast the marshmallows in the fire. If you have time to collect them."

"I'm a little stiff, but I can handle that," Melanie answered.

"Oh, no. Stiff from what? I knew something about your voice didn't sound right," Kevin said, his voice full of concern.

It felt good to know how much he cared. "Perfection took a fall today. It was awful!" Melanie wailed. Her voice caught in her throat. "I thought you probably heard about it from your dad."

"Maybe he doesn't know yet. He didn't say anything about it to me. How's Perfection?"

"It might be six months before he's better. Oh, Kevin, I rode terribly. I never really had control of him. And now he's hurt!" Melanie cried.

Kevin was quiet a moment. When he spoke, his voice was gentle. "There's not an exercise rider alive who hasn't lost control at some point, and you've just started. It's not your fault, Mel. What happened, anyway?"

"The vet said he has a pulled muscle."

Kevin's voice was soft. "That's not so bad, Mel. And six months isn't that long. He's only a two-year-old. Anyway, how are you? Did you get hurt? "

"I scraped up my arms, my face, and my left leg," she said, attempting a laugh. "And ripped a pair of jeans."

Kevin laughed, too. "Jeans. Now *that's* serious. I hope they weren't your best pair."

"Nope, just one of my favorites." Melanie giggled.

"Tough loss. I'll help you feel better about them if you hurry on over here," Kevin teased.

Melanie smiled. Kevin always made her feel better. "Yes, sir," she answered mockingly. "I'll get Christina and we'll get moving. Stick collecting first, sir. We should arrive by eighteen hundred hours."

Kevin laughed. "Okay. See you at six."

Melanie hung up the phone and sat at the table a moment before going to look for Christina. In the face of all her worries, Kevin had made her smile. She was really lucky to have him for a friend.

As they walked through the trees, looking for sticks suitable for roasting hot dogs and marshmallows, Melanie wondered when Christina would say something about her scrapes. Christina was acting as though everything were fine, but Melanie could feel the tension in the air between them.

Melanie had tied a bandanna around her head. It covered only the top of the long scrape on her forehead and face, but she hoped it would distract everyone's attention from her other injuries. She saw Christina staring at her head.

"Nice bandanna," she said finally.

"Thanks," Melanie said, unsure if Christina was teasing her or not.

Having a cookout to go to should have helped distract Melanie from her worries, but they kept coming back, no matter how hard she tried to brush them all away. Christina must have known about her fall on Perfection, but she wasn't letting on. Had she told Ashleigh that Melanie wasn't even supposed to be riding that morning?

The girls both bent to pick up the same stick, and Christina looked Melanie in the eye. "It doesn't hide the scrape," she said.

Melanie frowned and pulled the bandanna lower.

"Mom told me how it happened." She stared at Melanie. "That scrape looks terrible. Have you put anything on it?"

Melanie felt uncomfortable. Everyone at the bonfire would want to know what had happened, and she would have to tell them about the fall, and about Perfection getting hurt.

"Melanie, did you hear me? Have you put anything on that scrape?" Christina asked again.

Melanie touched her forehead gingerly. "Samantha put something on it. It's okay," she said.

Christina bent to pick up another stick. "Do you want to talk about it?" she asked.

"No. I don't even want to think about it," Melanie answered.

They walked a few steps in silence, then Christina asked, "What did Mom do about your dad's call? Did she talk to him yet?"

Melanie hesitated. "Um, I was going to . . . um . . . ," she muttered.

"You mean you didn't tell her?" Christina demanded, staring. "With everything that happened today?"

"I was going to tell her this morning before I rode, but then I thought I could get just one more ride in, and that maybe I could figure something out by then," Melanie admitted.

"How about after the spill? You still didn't tell her? Oh, Mel!" Christina scoffed.

"After the fall I couldn't. I mean, how could I tell Ashleigh that I wasn't supposed to ride, knowing full well that if I had listened to my dad, Perfection wouldn't be hurt?" Melanie sat down on a tree stump and put her head in her hands. "If I'd told her right away, Ashleigh would still trust me. Now when I do tell her she probably won't want me to ride ever again." Melanie rubbed her face. "I'm not even sure I *should* ride again," she mumbled.

Christina shook her head. Then she touched Melanie's shoulder in a way that let Melanie know she cared. "Let's get to the cookout before they wonder where we are," she said, her brow furrowed with worry.

The rest of the way they walked in silence. Melanie was worn out. She guessed Christina didn't know what else to say. She knew things still weren't right between them, but at least Christina had spoken to her. Melanie sighed. *I really messed things up*, she thought.

"Hey, guys," Katie yelled when she saw Melanie and Christina. She jumped up, the pink and blue checked lawn chair she'd been sitting in taking a nosedive. "How's it going? Ooh!" She drew back and looked at Melanie's face. "We heard about the fall. That looks pretty nasty!"

Melanie touched her face. "It's not as bad as it looks," she said slowly, wondering how much they had heard.

"It does look bad, but I'm glad you're okay," Cassidy added. "We heard you scraped your leg and arms, too."

Melanie held up both arms. Katie and Cassidy wrinkled their noses at the ugly red scrape that ran down her left arm, and the smaller, lighter one on her right arm.

"You just can't trust a two-year-old to stay on all four feet," Dylan joked.

Parker Townsend grinned. "You look a lot better

than I did after my big fall," he said, putting things in perspective. Parker had taken a nasty fall over a huge cross-country fence and broken his arm.

Melanie smiled grimly. Leave it to Parker to make her realize that it could have been worse. Melanie looked past Parker to Kevin, who was standing at the grill flipping burgers. She wondered how much he'd told them about Perfection's injury.

"We heard Perfection will be laid up for a while," Dylan added. "But like Kevin said, he'd have fallen no matter who was riding. It's you we were worried about."

Melanie flashed a grateful smile at Kevin, and he grinned back. He had a big white apron wrapped around him, and Melanie thought it made him look even cuter than usual. She thrust the sticks she'd collected into Cassidy's hands. "Here are the roasting sticks for the bonfire," she said. "Christina and I picked them up on the way over."

Christina held out the ones she'd collected.

"We miss you at Mona's," Katie said to Christina.

"I miss you all, too," Christina told them.

"How do you like taking lessons at Samantha's?" Cassidy asked.

"Sterling's going great, and Samantha is such a great teacher," Christina said. "I know I'm going to learn a lot."

"And she gets to see me," Parker joked. "That's the part she likes best."

While the attention was on Christina, Melanie slipped toward the smoking grill and Kevin. "Hey. How's it going?" she asked.

"I should be asking you that," Kevin said.

"No, you shouldn't," Melanie said, rolling her eyes. "Too many people are asking me that today."

Kevin put down the spatula. "I'm glad you're all right," he said, looking straight into her eyes.

Melanie looked away, embarrassed by the intensity of his gaze. "I'm fine," she said, pulling away slightly as Kevin's dad came out the kitchen door.

Ian McLean grinned as he put an arm across his son's shoulders. "You aren't burning those burgers, are you, Kev?" he asked.

"No, Dad," Kevin said, picking up the spatula again.

"Good. I just thought it was getting kind of hot over here," Ian joked.

"Dad!" Kevin's face turned red, and Melanie lowered her head and smiled. At that moment Kevin's mother, Beth, came out of the house carrying a tray laden with bowls of potato salad and coleslaw, and a pot of steaming baked beans.

Ian looked at Melanie. "I didn't tell Kevin about the fall. I thought you'd want to do it yourself."

"Thanks," Melanie said gratefully.

Ian pointed to the table piled with paper plates, napkins, plastic forks, rolls, and condiments. "Okay, gang, everything is ready," he announced. "Let's eat!"

After the flurry of plate gathering and standing in line to pile plates high, everyone settled at the picnic table, talking and laughing while they ate.

Ian and Beth gathered wood and carried it through the big yard, kneeling to build a small bonfire in a clearing away from the trees.

"Tomorrow's already Wednesday," Kevin groaned. "It's our last day off. Maybe we could all get together for a late afternoon trail ride."

"Sounds good to me," Cassidy said, munching on a potato chip.

Katie bit into her burger, nodding in agreement, and Dylan said, "I'm in." Soon everyone had agreed to meet at Mona's barn at four o'clock the next day.

"I can't wait for the yearling sale," Kevin said. "Mike and I have been training the yearlings to load into the trailer so they'll go easy for the sale."

"Yeah, but the yearling sale always reminds me that show season is almost over," Cassidy said sadly.

"I know, we only have two more shows," Katie added.

As the conversation turned toward the last shows of the season, Melanie let her mind wander. She swatted at a yellow jacket that buzzed near her soda can, but it buzzed back, even more determined than before. On the next swat her soda can tipped over, and the brown liquid rushed across the table and under Christina's plate.

Melanie grabbed the can and any napkins that

were nearby, swiping at the liquid that dripped through the cracks in the picnic table and onto Christina's jeans.

Christina leaped up, pulling her soggy plate with her, but the plate split in half as she lifted it, and her burger was pitched to the ground. "Melanie!" she shouted, dismayed.

"I'm sorry," Melanie sputtered as she rubbed Christina's jeans with the soggy napkins, trying to soak up the spill. Kevin had sprinted for the house, and now he rushed over with a roll of paper towels, wiping up the last of the puddle of soda.

Christina looked down at her sticky, wet jeans and back up at Melanie. "You are just an accident waiting to happen," she said, shaking her head. "Why can't you be more careful?"

Melanie stared at Christina. The words had hit her like a ton of bricks. *It's true*, she thought. *I am an accident waiting to happen* . . . again and again. First it had been Milky Way, and now Perfection. The spilled soda was just another reminder that she was bad luck. Melanie strode off toward the fire that was now blazing in the backyard.

Beth and Ian had headed toward the barns, hand in hand in the early darkness. The fire they'd built was contained by a ring of stones. Melanie stood quietly beside it, replaying the accident in her head. Perfection had just stumbled, hadn't he? But she hadn't been in control, so it was her fault, more or less. Then her

90

thoughts turned to Milky Way and she felt a terrible weight pressing down on her, turning her stomach to lead and her mind to mush. She had killed one horse, and now she'd hurt another. *But Perfection will be all right*, she thought. *As long as I'm not riding him.*

Melanie heard a sound beside her and turned to see Kevin. He put his arm around her shoulders. "It's not your fault," he told her softly. "It's not anyone's fault. It just happened." Melanie wondered if he could read her mind. It was as if he knew what she was thinking, what she was going through.

"But why did it have to happen at all?" she mumbled into his shoulder.

Kevin held her at arm's length, and she looked at him. He was still wearing the white apron, and now it looked ghostly in the flickering light of the campfire. The flames were reflected in his blue eyes as he gazed down at her, and Melanie's heart did a flip-flop.

"There doesn't have to be a reason," he said, so quietly that she barely heard him. "You're a good rider, and a good person. Please stop thinking that you're not."

Melanie repeated the words in her head, thankful that Kevin believed in her. She just wished she could make Christina believe in her, too.

7

IN THE MORNING ASHLEIGH CAME INTO MELANIE'S ROOM and shook her gently. "Did you forget? We're going to go to Keeneland today."

Melanie groaned. The race. She had forgotten. So much had happened since they'd discussed it the morning before. "Maybe I'll stay home and recuperate for one more day."

Ashleigh sat on the edge of the bed. "No, you won't. I'm not going to let you sit around all day feeling sorry for yourself. The only way to get better is to get going. I know Perfection is going to be okay, but I'm not so sure about you. I think you need a push. Now get up and come along with Ian and Sam and me. You can't spend your life worrying over what has already happened. You have to get on with things."

Melanie ran a finger down the sore part of her face, fighting back tears. "I don't know."

"What about Naomi?" Ashleigh added. "She needs you cheering for her in her first race." Ashleigh patted the blanket over Melanie's arm. "Now let's get going!"

Melanie stretched. "Okay. If Naomi needs me to cheer her on, then I'll be there," she agreed, and forced a smile.

In the barn, Samantha and Naomi were waiting. Faith's legs had already been wrapped in shipping bandages, and she was blanketed for the ride. The gray filly looked alert and eager, as if she knew this was her day. Ian backed up the Whitebrook horse van, and Ashleigh led Faith up the ramp and tied her inside. They piled into the cab and pulled out of the driveway just as the sun was peeking over the barn roofs. As they rumbled past Whisperwood on the right, Faith let out a lonely whinny.

"What's the strategy for the race?" Naomi asked.

"You want to conserve her energy," Ian instructed. "Faith likes to compete, so if she's challenged, she's going to want to be in the front. You'll have to hold her back, make her wait, or she'll burn out too fast."

Samantha was studying *Racing News*, an industry newspaper Ashleigh subscribed to. "And I think she will be challenged," she said. "I'm pretty sure Lethal Leopard is going to be running in this race."

"Hmmm." Ashleigh moved her hand down on the steering wheel. "Where did you hear that?" she asked.

"It's in an article about Fascination Farm. Listen to this. It says, 'Lethal Leopard may be one of the fastest fillies to come out of Fascination Farm. Outsiders will soon get a look at this amazing Thoroughbred's racing ability. Trainer Berkley Kern said Lethal Leopard would run in a September maiden race at Keeneland.' What do you think of that?"

Ashleigh's brow was furrowed in thought. "I've heard about Leopard. The amazing thing is that she doesn't have spectacular lines, but that filly can race," she said, shifting into high gear as they entered the highway.

Naomi sighed. "Thanks! I was feeling just fine. Now I'm worried," she said.

Samantha and Ashleigh laughed together. They knew what pre-race jitters felt like firsthand.

"There's no need to worry, Naomi," Ian said. "You know Faith. She's hot, too, but we haven't been out blowing our horn to the press about her."

"Whitebrook's best-kept secret," Melanie quipped.

"Just let Leopard lead the race," Ian said. "Let Faith save her energy. Keep her on Leopard's tail and then, *boom*, pass her in the backstretch!"

When Ian said "boom," Melanie jumped in her seat. Naomi giggled, and soon everyone was laughing. Melanie knew they were still a little nervous, but it felt good to laugh just the same.

*　　*　　*

After Faith was in her stall at the track, Samantha began grooming her. Ashleigh and Ian were giving Naomi more instructions, so Melanie ran to get a racing program. It was early and the betting area was quiet, so it was easy to get to the counter. Melanie knew the place would be teeming with people within the hour as the first races of the day were launched. As she walked back to the stabling area she leafed through the program, looking for the second race, Faith and Naomi's race. Sure enough, there was Lethal Leopard. Melanie glanced down the form. Several horses had been scratched. Besides Faith and Lethal Leopard, there were only three other fillies in the race, one called By-Cracky-Day, one named Cross Patch, and a filly called Senzational. Melanie hurried back to the shed row.

"Leopard is in the race," she announced as she rounded the corner.

Samantha was holding Faith's lead shank while Ian carefully examined the filly's legs.

"Great!" Naomi said, pacing in front of Faith's stall.

"Now don't get nervous," Ashleigh told Naomi. "Faith will pick up on it, and then your biggest problem will be holding her back!"

"I know, I know," Naomi said. She plopped down on a bale of straw outside of Faith's stall. "I'm being silly. Faith and I really have a connection. All I have to do is think about how she feels under me on the track, and how fast she's been our last few times out, and I know we'll be just fine." Naomi stood up again. Taking a deep breath, she smiled. "We're going to win," she announced.

Ian had Faith's left hind foot in his lap, picking it out. He looked up when Ashleigh spoke.

"If you don't win, it's still okay," Ashleigh said. "This race is experience for Faith . . . and for you," she added, and Ian nodded his agreement.

By the end of the first race Naomi looked completely calm. She listened carefully to Ian's last-minute instructions and accepted a leg up from Samantha. She high-fived Melanie before she mounted and made her way to the post parade.

Melanie leaned on the fence and watched them load Cross Patch into the number one slot. She saw Ashleigh walking around the track toward her. Ian would lead Faith into the starting gate. But first Lethal Leopard was loaded into the number two gate. She was a leggy black mare with two white socks on her forelegs. She was tall and sleek, and her conformation spelled speed. The Leopard was followed in the starting gates by By-Cracky-Day. Faith had drawn the number four gate. Melanie knew Naomi would have preferred to be on the rail, but she had accepted the luck of the draw without a word. Now, as Melanie watched, Faith walked calmly into the gate. Then they were ready to load Senzational into the last gate. Ashleigh and Ian joined Melanie at the rail.

"My fingers are crossed," she told them, holding up both hands.

"Mine too," Ashleigh said. "It's a bare-bones race," she said, "and that's a good way for Naomi to start."

"What do you mean?" Melanie asked.

"If one more horse had been scratched, they would have called off the race," Ashleigh explained. "Five horses is a small race."

Melanie looked up again, and her heart pounded as she watched Senzational fighting, rearing, refusing to load into the last gate. The chestnut filly looked wild, out of control. Next to her, Faith was beginning to prance, and Melanie could see the sweat darkening her neck.

"Come on," Ashleigh mumbled. "Get that mare in before Faith gets too fired up."

As if on cue, Senzational walked in. Melanie leaned on the rail, watching intently. She could feel her heartbeat throbbing against the rail. Then the buzzer rang out and the doors flew open. Five horses burst from the gate.

Ian had both elbows on the fence. He was leaning in, watching every move.

Come on, Faith. Come on, Naomi, Melanie thought. She strained her eyes against the backdrop of bright blue sky, watching as Lethal Leopard and Leap of Faith pulled away from the pack, moving in unison, taking an immediate lead of a length, now two, now three. When Melanie blinked, Leopard surged ahead by another half length.

"No!" Melanie said out loud, and she felt Ashleigh's arm come around her shoulder and grip it tightly.

"It's okay, Mel," she said. "Naomi is holding her back the way Ian told her to. They're right where they should be. Sometimes strategy wins over speed. Remember the turtle and the hare?"

Melanie smiled, but she could see that Faith was fighting Naomi. Faith hated being behind another horse. Having Lethal Leopard so near only made it worse. The filly pulled at the bit, and as she watched, Melanie could tell the very moment Faith gained control. Faith took the bit in her teeth and Naomi leaned forward, as if she knew it wouldn't do any good to fight. Melanie had felt the same way riding Perfection the day before. It was the first time all day she'd let a reminder of her fall enter her thoughts, and she quickly swept it away as she watched Faith soar past Leopard, a full length ahead of the flashy black filly.

"It's too soon," Ashleigh groaned. "She'll never hold the lead now. She's going to burn out before the finish line."

Ian had his foot up on the fence rail now, and Melanie could tell his entire focus was on Faith and Naomi.

Melanie stayed silent. She didn't want to think that Faith would lose. But as they came sweeping down the backstretch she could see Ashleigh's prediction materializing before her eyes. Leopard was gaining again, bearing down on Faith with a vengeance. As they shot under the wire the pair were neck and neck, nose to nose, in a photo finish.

"Did she win?" Melanie's eyes were wide as she stared at Ashleigh.

"I don't know. It was too close to call."

Ian spun around. "We'll have to wait for the steward's decision," he said.

Faith was rounding the track. Naomi turned her back toward home, letting the mare canter out her last bit of energy. Melanie saw the board was flashing Photo Finish in bold yellow letters. Her heart was beating in time with the flash of the lights. She followed Ashleigh and Ian, walking numbly toward the paddock area where Faith would emerge. Just as Faith came into the paddock the announcer boomed, "The winner of race number two, in a photo finish, is Leap of Faith, owned by Whitebrook Farm, trained by Ashleigh Griffin and Samantha McLean, Naomi Traeger up."

Melanie let out a whoop that made Faith step back in surprise. She grabbed her aunt around the waist in a huge hug. "We did it," she shouted. "I mean, you did it!" she added, looking up at Naomi. "And you!" She patted Faith's neck awkwardly. The filly was blowing, her nostrils flared pink.

Ian helped Naomi dismount and took Faith's reins.

"You really did do it," Samantha told Naomi. "Faith challenged you, but you handled it well."

"Nice riding," Ashleigh added, beaming.

"Excellent," Ian said, a huge smile stretched across his face.

Everyone was smiling as they led Faith into the winner's circle for pictures. "Come here, Melanie," Ashleigh said. "You get in this one, too." She pulled Melanie into the picture. As the photographer's camera clicked, Melanie wondered if she would ever be in Naomi's position, riding a winning horse.

Everyone was all talked out by the time they loaded Faith for the ride home. Samantha offered to drive, and Ashleigh seemed grateful to hand her the keys. They rode a good way in silence. Naomi laid her head back on the seat and fell asleep.

"She deserves a rest," Samantha said quietly, and Ashleigh agreed.

Then Ashleigh said, "Melanie, I think I want you up on Stone on Saturday."

Melanie's mind went blank. "I . . . I d-don't think I'm ready to ride yet," she stuttered.

"You have the rest of the week to recover," Ashleigh said.

"B-But . . . ," Melanie stuttered. She knew she had to tell Ashleigh what her father had said, but she just couldn't bring herself to do it.

"The sooner you get back on board, the easier it will be," Ian said.

"Yes. You're almost better now." Ashleigh lightly touched Melanie's face, which was healing. "It'll be good for you to get back into the swing of things right away. You can't dwell on what happened," she insisted.

Melanie looked down at her hands, rubbing one thumb over the other anxiously. How could she tell her aunt that she was not supposed to be riding? How could she tell her that she was not even supposed to ride the day Perfection was hurt?

"Believe me, Mel, it's best," Ashleigh said, and finally Melanie nodded.

They were almost home when Melanie remembered the trail ride. By the time she helped unload Faith and excused herself, it was almost five o'clock. She raced to tack up Trib. *I'll meet them on the trail*, she thought.

Trib seemed surprised to see Melanie. He had just stood up from a wonderfully dusty roll. Melanie groaned. "You had to do that, didn't you?" she asked the pinto. Trib shook his whole body, spraying Melanie with dirt.

Melanie hooked a lead shank to the pony and led him from the field. In the barn, she put him in crossties and started grooming out the dust and dirt. She moved quickly, her thoughts racing. *Christina's going to be so angry at me*, she thought. *She'll say this proves her point.*

Melanie swished away the dust on Trib's back, then lifted each hoof to pick out the muck inside. Next she ran to the tack room to get the saddle and bridle, racing back again when she realized she had forgotten to grab the reins, which had been detached for cleaning.

Finally she was ready to go. She put on her helmet, mounted the pony, and headed toward Mona's. She'd cut across the field and meet them on the wooded trail, she reasoned. But as she crested the hill she saw Christina, on Sterling Dream, and Kevin, on Jasper, trotting toward her. Kevin lifted his hand and waved.

"Hi, Melanie!" Kevin called as he slowed. "I didn't want to leave without you. I waited forever, but it looked like you wouldn't make it home in time."

"She didn't," Christina said dourly.

"Is it over?" Melanie asked.

Christina rolled her eyes. "Of course it's over. It's about to get dark."

"Maybe we can go again tomorrow," Kevin suggested.

"It's a school day," Christina reminded him.

"Maybe Saturday morning, then," Kevin insisted.

"I can't," Melanie said miserably. "I promised Ashleigh I'd ride Stone Saturday morning."

"You're riding again?"

"I know, I know." Melanie felt her chest tighten. "I'm going to tell her. I am!"

"Tell who what?" Kevin looked confused.

"Two days ago her father forbade her to ride on the track," Christina said. "She was supposed to tell my mom to call him. But she didn't."

"And I'm still riding," Melanie finished for her. She looked at Kevin, hoping he'd understand. "I'm so afraid my dad's going to make me stop permanently."

Melanie stroked Trib's neck. "I know I want to be a jockey one day, so I can't just give it up. It's all I want to do. Today, watching Naomi ride, I was more certain than ever," she declared.

Christina shook her head. "But you're going be in even bigger trouble if you don't tell my mom," she warned.

Melanie stared at Christina. She was so confused. Why did Christina get so angry whenever she brought up riding on the track? "I just wish you could understand," she said. Then she turned Trib and galloped toward home.

8

MELANIE SPENT LITTLE TIME IN THE BARNS ON THURSDAY and Friday. She slept later than usual each day, then hurried to school and home again. When she checked on Perfection and visited with Pirate she kept it short, using homework as an excuse. But her heart was torn with the desire to be in the barns and riding again. She knew what the real problem was: She needed to talk to Ashleigh, but staying away gave her an excuse not to do it.

Melanie got up extra early on Saturday. She hadn't slept well. Now she just wanted to check on Perfection. She padded downstairs in jeans and an oversized T-shirt, stopping in the kitchen for a glass of orange juice and a cold bagel. She stuffed a carrot in her pocket, and munched on the bagel as she walked toward the barn in complete darkness.

Perfection was lying down when she got there. He lifted his sleepy head and snorted, then struggled to stand. He'd gotten good at maneuvering around the injured leg, using his other three legs for balance. He stared at Melanie, his mane peppered with sawdust sprinkles, then shook like a wet dog emerging from a cold pond. His mane landed smoothly, lying in even layers.

"Hi, boy," Melanie said to the elegant chestnut. "How are you feeling today?" The horse chuffed in response. "Come on over here," she said, offering him the carrot.

Perfection nudged her outstretched hand, crunching the treat between his teeth. After the last bite he turned his back on her and went to the corner of his stall to check his feed bucket for any stray bits of grain.

"You'll get your feed in a little while," Melanie promised him. "But first let's hose your leg." She opened the door and stepped inside. Clipping a lead shank to the colt's halter, she led him out of the barn and toward the wash racks. She watched him walk, observing his step, trying to see if he was putting any more weight on the injured leg. He lifted the injured leg carefully and put it down even more particularly, letting the good foreleg take the weight.

She tied Perfection in the wash rack and turned the hose on his bad leg. It was still swollen just above the knee joint, and when she touched the puffy area, it felt hot and full of fluid. She turned the water to a slow stream so the pressure wouldn't aggravate the sore muscle. As the cool water ran over his leg, Perfection leaned against the wash rack patiently, as though he knew that what she was doing would help.

Melanie let her thoughts wander as she hosed Perfection's leg. She felt miserable. If only she'd been up front with her aunt from the start and told her about her dad's call, Perfection wouldn't be hurt at all, since she wouldn't have ridden that day. And maybe Ashleigh would have helped her work something out with her father. Now it was probably too late.

Melanie put away the hose, deciding that she couldn't wait another day. She'd tell her aunt the whole truth this morning, *before* she was supposed to ride. It was too hard to walk around with this lump of guilt inside. She walked Perfection back to his stall and fed him his grain, then headed toward the other barn. Samantha was inside, tacking up Stone for his early morning exercise.

"There you are!" Sam exclaimed.

"Hi, Sam. Where's Ashleigh?" Melanie asked.

"She's going to be late today. She and Ian are going over the yearling list with Mike one more time. She said this morning was the only time they could get their schedules to mesh. She wants to double-check her choices with him. But she told me to tell you we should go ahead without her," Sam explained.

"Oh," Melanie said, fidgeting. "I kind of wanted to talk to her before I rode today."

"Anything I can help you with?" Samantha asked as she pulled Stone's girth tight. When he blew out his breath she put her knee against him and buckled the girth in the correct hole.

"No, I just . . . ," Melanie began, fumbling for the words.

"Mel, I know you're nervous about today's ride—it's always tough to get on after a fall. But you'll be fine, don't worry," Sam assured her.

"It's not that," Melanie countered.

"Honest, I'm going to go real easy on you both today. He only needs a light workout. No galloping, just a light canter to loosen up the joints and keep his muscles in shape," Sam said.

"Okay, Sam," Melanie said, and forced a smile. "Never mind—it was something else, anyway. You're right, I'll be fine." She moved to pat Stone's neck, her mind busy with worry.

"We won't have him going in the starting gate today," Samantha went on. "He gets fractious when we work him in the gate too much."

"That sounds fine," Melanie agreed before changing the subject. "Have you looked at Perfection lately?"

"Just this morning," Sam told her.

"Does he look any better to you?" Melanie asked.

"A lot better. He still has that swelling in the morning, but I expect that will go down again by afternoon. We're waiting for the swelling to disappear altogether.

Then we'll know he's better." She eyed Melanie and sighed good-naturedly. "It won't be long, so stop worrying," she said. "The vet said it could be as long as six months, but he's already healing faster than we expected. I think he'll be back to feeling like himself a lot sooner than that."

They walked to the track together, leading Stone between them. In the distance Melanie saw a hay truck, loaded to the top, creeping up the long driveway to Whitebrook. It seemed strange not to have Ashleigh along. Samantha gave Melanie a leg up and a reassuring smile.

Melanie jogged Stone out to the quarter pole. He was on his best behavior, and she was grateful. Her stomach lurched every time she thought about her last ride and Perfection's fall. At the red and white striped pole she turned for home and let him canter, careful not to give him his head. Her legs, her hands, her whole demeanor told the big bay that he would not get away with anything on this day, and he didn't try to.

As they cantered back toward the wire Melanie relaxed some. This was what she loved—feeling the surge of power beneath her, moving as fast as the wind, smelling the earthy track, feeling the warm sun on her back. It was a relief to be riding on the track again.

"Excellent workout!" Samantha said, and took Stone's reins. Melanie couldn't stop herself from smiling as she dismounted, patting the bay's solid neck.

But when she turned around, Ashleigh was striding toward them, and the look on her aunt's face was grim.

"Melanie, Christina tells me that your father forbade you to ride on the track," she announced. "Days ago. Is that true?"

Melanie's heart sank, and she stared at the dusty toes of her paddock boots. "Yes," she answered quietly. "I meant to tell you. . . ."

"Now I know why his number has been on our caller ID four times in the past three days! I'd been trying to catch him in but didn't succeed until this morning, *after* I talked to Christina. He'll be here tomorrow."

Melanie gulped, swallowing another lame excuse. She couldn't stand the disappointment in Ashleigh's voice. How could she have messed everything up so badly? "I really wanted to tell you, but . . . "

"I know you wanted to exercise-ride, Melanie, but I am very upset with you." She took Stone's bridle and began to walk him toward the barn. Samantha walked beside her, and Melanie trailed behind.

"I'm sorry, Sam," Melanie heard her aunt say. "Until we sort things out, I can't let her ride anymore."

As she walked down the hill toward the barns, Melanie felt the weight of her mistake pressing down on her, and her shoulders began to shake as she sobbed. Ashleigh hadn't mentioned Perfection's injury, but Melanie knew she had to be thinking that if Melanie had followed her father's orders, the colt would still be sound. When her father came, he would see her

109

scratches and Perfection's leg and be even more upset. He might even want to take her back to New York!

Then Melanie had a terrible thought. This was all Christina's fault! If Melanie had had a chance to tell Ashleigh herself, maybe things would be different. *How could she tell on me like that?* Melanie wondered.

But in her heart Melanie knew it hadn't been fair to burden her cousin with such a big secret. It was just as bad as asking Christina to lie to her own mother. *Oh, what have I done?* Melanie thought miserably.

Taking a deep breath, she continued toward the barn, feeling more alone than she had since Milky Way's death. Ashleigh and Samantha had already disappeared inside with Stone. Melanie wandered down the hill, then set her sights on the broodmare barn. It was a safe zone, a place where she was unlikely to meet up with Christina. Melanie was too furious to take a chance of running into her cousin now. She needed to be alone to think things through.

The air in the barn was sweet, with the smell of fresh hay and straw. Each stall was piled high with a thick bed of clean straw. Perfect Heart was standing with her nose down, pawing the bedding and rooting for stray strands of hay.

Melanie opened the stall door and stepped inside. She put her head down on the mare's side and breathed deeply. "Hi, girl," she said softly, then she was sobbing again, letting out all the anger, sadness, pain, and guilt that had built up over the past few days. "I really messed up this time," she told the mare. "I feel so bad."

Perfect Heart munched on a piece of hay, turning her head to look at Melanie. Her belly had expanded even more, and Melanie ran her hand over it as she spoke. "Ashleigh's mad at me, and my dad's angry, too. On top of all that, I put Christina in a spot where she had to keep a big secret, and I guess that wasn't fair to her, either," Melanie whispered as she rubbed Heart's underbelly. "Worst of all," she said in a broken voice, pausing to wipe away a tear, "I hurt your baby— Perfection is lame because of stupid, stubborn me!" Melanie buried her head in Heart's mane. Heart stood quietly, her gentle, patient expression providing a sort of motherly comfort to the distraught girl.

Melanie was silent at dinner that evening, careful to avoid any eye contact with Christina or Ashleigh. After dinner she sat in her room and fretted over what she would do. Her dad would arrive the next day. By then no one would be speaking to her. As she stretched out on her bed and thought about it all, she accepted the fact that she had put Christina in a very sticky predicament. It had been very wrong of her to expect Christina to keep a secret from her mother.

It was past eight o'clock when she walked down the hall to Christina's room. Christina was lying across her bed, just as Melanie had been.

"Can I come in?" Melanie asked timidly.

111

Christina looked up and then rolled over, pulling a pillow over her eyes as if trying to hide the fact that she'd been crying, too. "Sure," she answered, her voice muffled.

Melanie sat at the bottom of Christina's bed and fiddled with her fingers a moment before speaking. "I'm so sorry," she admitted.

Christina sat up, looking stunned. "*You're* sorry?" she cried, her eyes wide. "But I'm the one who should apologize! You aren't angry at me?" she demanded.

Melanie's emotions were so close to the surface that she had to take a breath in order not to start crying all over again. "I wish you hadn't told your mom," she said, "but it was wrong of me to put you in the middle of it."

"No, I shouldn't have said anything," Christina insisted, rubbing her eyes. "And the truth is, I only did it because I was angry at you. I wanted my mom to be mad at you," she admitted.

Melanie felt a prick of hurt, but she shoved it aside. They were so close to working things out. Relief was written all over Christina's face, and Melanie felt as though a heavy weight had been lifted off her, too. It felt so good to be talking again. "But why were you so mad?" she asked.

Christina wiped away another tear, but more followed, running down her cheeks. "I've always felt like I let my mom down by not wanting to learn to exercise-ride. I always used the excuse that I'll probably be too big to be a jockey anyway, but I know my mom was disappointed. Now you're doing it, and my mom is like your best friend or something. She spends every morning with you, and she talks about what a great rider you are all the time. It's like *you* are what she wanted *me* to be, and I couldn't take it!" Christina sobbed. "I know it's stupid," she said, tears streaming down her face, "but I was so jealous of you, and I refused to admit it, even to myself."

Melanie scooted closer to Christina on the bed. She touched Christina's arm. "It wasn't just you," she admitted. "I guess I was enjoying all the attention just a little too much. For the first time I felt like I was good at something, and somebody was noticing it. But I didn't pay attention to how you were feeling. And I should have," she said.

"Well, I should have talked to you right from the start," Christina insisted. "It was stupid of me to let it all build up inside until I could burst."

Melanie looked down at her feet. "It's okay," she said. " I guess we were just confused. But I'm still in a lot of trouble," she finished with a sigh.

"We'll work it out," Christina promised. She wrapped an arm around Melanie, and Melanie hugged her cousin back.

"It doesn't matter anymore," Melanie said finally. "My dad is on his way here, and he won't let me ride after he hears what happened." She took a tissue out of the box on Christina's dresser and blew her nose. "I'll be lucky if he doesn't make me go back to New York," she choked out, struggling to control a fresh bout of sobs. "I really blew it this time."

Christina reached for a tissue, too. She blew her nose and attempted a smile, catching Melanie's eye. "Don't worry, Mel. We'll come up with something to change your dad's mind. I promise," she said.

9

MELANIE AWOKE EARLY SUNDAY MORNING WITH A LUMP IN her throat. Her eyes were red and puffy from all the crying she'd done the night before, and she felt achy and awful. She forced herself to get out of bed, wash, and dress. She wanted to get to the barn. *It might be my last time*, she told herself, *if Dad decides to drag me back to New York.*

First she went to check on Perfection. He was standing with his head over the stall door. She rubbed his velvety neck affectionately. He snorted and tossed his head, looking for a treat. Melanie smiled. "None today, big guy," she said. Just down the aisle she found a pitchfork and a muck bucket. She opened the stall door and went inside. The leggy chestnut watched her pick the manure and wet sawdust from his stall. Then she gave him his morning grain. "I'll be back later today to hose your leg," she promised Perfection as she moved down the aisle.

Pirate seemed happy to see her. Once inside his stall, she leaned against him for a long time, hugging his neck for comfort. He stood still. It was as though he understood that she needed him. Melanie realized that she missed the amount of time they'd been spending together before she'd begun exercising the horses, and it hit her that at least she'd still have Pirate if her dad made her stop riding the racehorses. *That is, if he doesn't make me move back to New York City,* she added to herself ruefully. Pirate nuzzled her gently when she came back to his stall with a tote full of grooming tools. She rooted around in the bucket, pulling out a currycomb and rubbing it over his coat in circular motions. As soon as the dust and grime had risen to the surface, she flicked it away with a dandy brush until his coat was clean and glossy. One by one she hand-picked pieces of hay and wood shavings from the silky black strands of his mane and tail. When she was done, Pirate leaned his big head against her, and she put her face against his. "I wonder if you still dream about racing," she murmured. "I bet you miss the track a lot more than I ever will. At least I still have a chance."

Before going to the house to clean up and face the family at breakfast, Melanie nipped into the broodmare barn to check on Perfect Heart. Kevin had said the mare was getting close to delivery. *Maybe it'll come soon*, she thought. Melanie took a deep breath as she stepped into the barn, breathing the warm smell of straw and horses, savoring it. The fourth stall down was Perfect Heart's. She heard a rustling before she reached the stall, and saw Heart circling when she drew near.

"Heart?" Melanie said. The mare looked up, startled, then circled again and lay down, groaning as she did.

Heart was about to give birth! Melanie sprinted down the aisle, out of the barn, and up the drive to the house. "It's Heart," she yelled as she ran, but her voice echoed emptily on the breeze. "Heart is about to foal!" she shouted again just outside the door.

Ashleigh came out of the kitchen holding a spatula, with Mike at her side. Christina dashed down the stairs just as Melanie announced again, "Heart is about to foal!"

"Come on, let's go," Ashleigh cried. She dropped the spatula and bolted toward the barn. Christina, Melanie, and Mike were close behind her.

"What was she doing?" Christina asked excitedly as they ran.

"She was circling in her stall. Then she lay down and kind of groaned like something was wrong," Melanie explained breathlessly.

"Nothing's wrong," Mike reassured Melanie. "That's all part of the process."

"But it's good that you came to get us," Ashleigh

added. She touched Melanie's shoulder. "You're about to see a foal be born."

Melanie felt a nervous shiver run down her spine as they rushed down the aisle of the broodmare barn. "Wow," she said. It was all she could manage.

"Don't worry, Mel. It's kind of scary at first, but it's really amazing, too," Christina reassured her.

When they reached the stall, Heart was down. It looked like the foal was ready to come out at any minute.

"I'll get the supplies," Mike called before racing to the tack room. Ashleigh opened the door of the stall and stepped quietly inside.

"Dad's getting iodine for the navel stump, and some rags to dry the newborn off," Christina whispered to Melanie as they hovered by the stall door.

"We've got a problem," Ashleigh called, her voice laced with concern. "She's too close to the wall. We need to move her over, or the wall will break the foal's neck when it comes out." She looked up and her eyes locked on Christina. "Come on, Chris. Help me move her," she said.

Christina made her way into the stall and stood in front of Heart's outstretched forelegs, waiting for Ashleigh's instructions. The contractions came in waves, easily identified by the ripple that ran through Heart's body, and the tenseness that followed. Her body was covered in a fine coat of sweat, and her eyes rolled with each contraction.

"We'll pull her to the right," Ashleigh told Christina. She took one of Heart's forelegs in her hands and motioned for Christina to take the other. "We'll pull between contractions," she instructed.

Melanie leaned against the door of the stall, trying to stay out of the way. Her heart thudded with worry as she watched. Heart's body was tense with anticipation as she waited for the next painful contraction. When it had come and gone, Christina and Ashleigh tugged the mare's front legs, struggling to move her body. Heart slid about six inches away from the wall. The mare flattened her ears and rolled her eyes, but she didn't put up a fight. A few moments later another contraction went through her.

"Here come the feet," Ashleigh said grimly. "We don't have time to waste! We've got to move her again, whether she's contracting or not."

The foal's forefeet were emerging. Together Christina and Ashleigh pulled Heart's legs once more. She slid another six inches away from the wall, and just in time, too, for the foal was coming fast now, hooves first, head down, like a diver. It was shrouded in a gauzy white sac that began to tear as the foal broke free. At that moment Mike rushed in with a bucket. He stood beside Melanie and watched.

Melanie felt as though she were seeing a movie on a screen. It didn't seem real to her. The rest of the sac tore and the foal came out in a rush of amniotic fluid. Heart immediately lifted her head and began to sniff her newborn.

"It's a filly," Ashleigh murmured.

The baby was wet and grayish brown. She had soft white hooves, and when her eyes fluttered open, Melanie thought she looked like Bambi—a tiny wet fawn.

"Perfect," Mike whispered.

Christina stooped down and rubbed Heart's neck. "Good girl," she said soothingly. "You have a pretty baby."

Ashleigh was moving aside the sac when Heart snorted and began to stand. Christina and Ashleigh jumped back, both of them smiling. "We did it, sweetie," Ashleigh said. She put her arm around Christina and pulled her close. "Thanks for helping."

Heart heaved herself to her feet, and the umbilical cord tore away, one short piece hanging in a stump from the foal's belly. Mimicking her mother, the foal immediately struggled to stand, scrambling up on two wobbly front legs, and then nose-diving into the hay.

Melanie had an overwhelming urge to help. She wanted to rush forward and hold the little one so she wouldn't fall again. But she knew better than to interfere. She'd heard Ashleigh talk about foaling many times before, and how important it was to let nature follow its course. They watched together as the foal tried to stand again and again, until finally she made it up and stood blinking at them, legs splayed.

"She's beautiful," Ashleigh whispered, as if she didn't want to break the spell that had settled over mother and baby. Heart touched noses with her new-born, looking as surprised as the filly. She snorted and began to lick the foal's nose, then its neck.

Melanie felt tears prick at her eyes, and she wiped them away. She glanced from the foal to Christina, who was wrapped in her mother's arms. She was glad to see the two of them sharing such a special moment.

The foal was trembling slightly as her mother licked her all over. Mike handed Christina a white towel from the bucket, and she began to dry the new-born so she wouldn't catch cold. Ashleigh took the iodine Mike poured into a tiny cup, and stooped down beside the foal to dip the umbilical stump.

Mike grinned and handed Melanie another towel. "Go ahead," he said. "Get to know her. Heart is used to this. We always bond with the foals at birth."

Melanie took the towel and moved forward slowly. She didn't want to startle Heart, but the mare didn't seem to mind the company surrounding her. She was too absorbed with her new baby, making grumbling sounds of satisfaction as she touched the filly's nose again.

"Hey," Christina said as she wiped mucus from the filly's little face. "She has a heart on her forehead, just like her mother!"

Melanie looked, and sure enough the heart was there. It wasn't neat and perfect like her mother's, but slightly jagged around the edges—a rough heart.

"It looks like the hearts you used to draw for me

121

on Valentine's Day when you were little," Ashleigh said to Christina. "Of course, they always looked perfect to me."

Melanie heard the stall door open and glanced up to see Kevin. "Hey," he said. "Now I know why Mike was running around like a maniac." He looked at the baby. "She's cute." He smiled at Melanie. "You were right, Mel. She's got your heart."

"Her heart?" Christina asked, raising her eyebrows.

"Oh, we were betting on the foal's markings, and I said the foal would have a heart on its forehead like Perfect Heart does," Melanie explained, blushing a little.

Just then Ashleigh touched Christina's elbow. "Foaling always makes me feel all emotional," Ashleigh said, and sighed. "Let's get out of here before I cry."

Christina smiled, scrunching up the towel in her hand.

"You know, when you were born, I did cry," Ashleigh continued. "You were so beautiful." She pointed a thumb at Perfect Heart and her newborn. "Let's leave them alone for a while. And we've got to come up with a good name, too."

Kevin, Melanie, Christina, and Ashleigh followed Mike out of the stall. Mike hurried off to find Ian, and Melanie and Kevin headed down the aisle side by side.

"Mom?" Melanie heard Christina say behind her. "We have to talk."

Melanie smiled, feeling better than she had in days.

Kevin tousled her hair. "With your psychic ability, you should call yourself Madam Mel and charge for predictions!" he joked.

Melanie laughed and punched his arm. After witnessing such an amazing spectacle and with Kevin there to make her smile, Melanie was almost convinced that everything would be all right after all.

Melanie's father was due to arrive early that evening. After lunch Christina and Melanie met Kevin in the broodmare barn. They leaned over the stall's half door to look at the new filly. "She's a chestnut, just like Pride," Melanie said. "When she was wet she looked sort of mousy, but her coat is clean and fluffy now."

"Yeah, they always look different once they dry off," Christina said. "She really does look like Pride, doesn't she?"

"Except for the heart," Kevin remarked.

"What do you think your mom will name her?" Melanie asked.

"She's already thinking about Pride's Heart. But she wants to wait to get to know the filly before deciding on a name for sure," Christina answered.

"That's a good name," Melanie said, and smiled as the foal sidled close to Heart and started to suckle. "The way she stood up right away took a lot of heart."

"They don't always get up that quickly," Christina agreed. "Maybe that was the first sign that she's going to be a great racehorse. Mona and Mom always say the most important ingredient in a horse's performance is heart."

"Is everything okay with you and your mom now?" Melanie asked.

Christina paused. "Well, we talked a lot," she said. "I've been worrying too much. My mom loves me for who I am. I guess I needed to hear her tell me that, and she did." She smiled. "Things are fine," she finished, and shrugged.

Kevin leaned closer to Melanie, his chin barely grazing the back of her head, his chest bumping her shoulder. Christina eyed the two of them suspiciously, and Melanie jumped away.

"What am I going to do about my dad?" she said, to hide her embarrassment. It was a topic she had avoided thinking about all day.

"When is he going to be here?" Christina asked.

"I don't know. Soon," Melanie said anxiously.

Christina and Kevin looked at each other. "You tell her," he said.

Melanie's head shot up. "Tell me what?" she demanded urgently. They were obviously up to something.

"We have a plan. You'll be taking a chance of getting in bigger trouble, but it just might work," Christina explained.

"Trouble's my middle name," Melanie said with a sigh. Just the thought of a bold new scheme to keep her father from making her stop riding on the track was enough to make her tingle all over with excitement. "What do I have to lose?"

Christina and Kevin's eyes met once again. Then Kevin nodded. "Let's do it," he said.

"Do what?" Melanie demanded, nudging Kevin with her elbow.

Kevin lowered his head to tell Melanie the plan that he and Christina had hatched. She nodded eagerly, and a moment later she hurried off to the barn with Kevin while Christina sprinted for the house to leave a note on the table.

10

"BOY, AM I GOING TO BE IN TROUBLE IF THIS DOESN'T work," Melanie said as they led Stone from his stall. "What makes you think my dad will be convinced?"

Kevin ran a hand through his hair. "Even if the man doesn't know horses, he's not blind. He'll see how happy you are on Stone. He'll see that you can control him, and how well you ride him."

Melanie brushed Stone's coat. "You guys sure have a lot of faith in me," she said gratefully.

"Yes, we do," Kevin agreed, smiling.

When he turned his eyes to her, Melanie looked away. *How can he be so nice to me?* she wondered. Stone pawed restlessly in the crossties while Kevin grabbed a brush and began working on Stone's other side.

Melanie lost herself in the grooming, currying out the dirt hidden deep inside Stone's dark bay coat. She was glad Kevin didn't say anything else flattering. She wasn't sure she'd know how to handle it.

"Earth to Melanie," Kevin said after several minutes, tossing a rag at Melanie. "Unlike you, I have no psychic abilities. What's up?"

Melanie was focused on Stone's coat. "Stone's got to look good," she said, laughing and tossing the rag back at him. "So quit fooling around. We've got to get this guy ready," she scolded.

Kevin shook his head. "Man, you're all work and no play."

"That's right. Now, how will we know when to go to the track?" she asked. "This has to be timed really well if it's going to work."

"Christina is going to ring the dinner bell when your dad arrives," Kevin explained.

"Won't that look suspicious?" Melanie asked.

"She said she'd do it like she was just fooling around with the bell. She'll pull it off fine. They'll be heading into the house for coffee, the way they always do when your dad first gets here, and that's when they'll find the note to meet you at the training track," Kevin said.

Melanie pulled a comb through Stone's black mane. "It might just work," she said, but she couldn't keep the worry from edging into her mind.

"That's the spirit. It will work. Think positive," Kevin coaxed.

"Or it might get me grounded for life." She groaned. "Get the saddle out for me, will you?"

"But of course, madam," Kevin said, and bowed.

"Stop teasing me, Kevin," Melanie ordered. "My stomach is in knots. I can't think funny right now."

"I noticed." Kevin pulled the tiny racing saddle from its rack in the tack room next to Stone's stall, threw it over his arm, and strode back toward her. "But I have to keep trying. It's my job to get your spirits up," he said smiling.

"Says who?" she asked.

"Says Christina." Kevin said.

"Oh." Melanie was surprised. Christina really was trying to fix things.

Gong! Gong! Gong! Kevin and Melanie heard the bell and froze. Then Melanie smoothed the saddle pad down on Stone's back and Kevin plopped the saddle on top. In one swift motion, Melanie pulled the girth under Stone's belly and buckled it before Stone could even think about bloating himself.

"The bridle—where is it?" she asked desperately.

"I don't know which one is his. There are at least twenty in there!" Kevin said, waving his hands in the air.

"Watch him," Melanie called as she raced into the tack room. She grabbed Stone's bridle and ran back. Stone seemed to sense her urgency and lowered his head to accept the bit. "Let's go!" Melanie said, her voice quivering as she pulled on Stone's reins and led him out the back of the barn. "If we go behind the barns and around that way, they won't see us until they get to the track."

"My thoughts exactly," Kevin said, and followed her out the door.

They had only gone a short way when Christina ran up. "Hey, you guys," she called excitedly. "Mel, when your dad came up the steps, I acted like I was fooling around and said, 'Announcing the famous record producer, Will Graham,' and then I rang the bell as if it were for him."

"And he ate it up, right?" Melanie smiled, thinking of her father. She was beginning to have second thoughts about their scheme. Should she just put Stone back in his stall and forget the whole thing? "Are they on their way down here yet?" she asked her cousin.

"They were heading into the house when I took off." Christina paused and took a couple of deep breaths. "They've probably read the note by now, so I guess they'll be here any minute."

"Maybe we shouldn't do this after all." Melanie said. She felt shaky.

"Hey, I've always thought of you as Ms. Nerves of Steel," Kevin said. "Don't disappoint me now."

"Sorry, but I can't help it. What if Stone stumbles, like Perfection did?"

"That won't happen," Christina said. "You have to ride, and you have to ride your best ever."

By the time they reached the training track, Christina, Kevin, and Melanie could see Ashleigh and Mike walking up the hill with Melanie's father.

Melanie's stomach was in knots and her mind raced. *What if this only makes matters worse?* she asked herself. But inside she knew she had to do it. She had to prove to her father, and to herself, that she was perfectly capable of riding the Thoroughbreds.

"Give me a leg up," she told Kevin. He cupped his hands and hoisted her into the saddle. She adjusted her riding helmet, tightening the chin strap.

"You look good up there," Christina said. "You can do it, Mel."

"Thanks, Christina," Melanie replied, grateful for her cousin's vote of confidence. Then, before she headed for the starting gate, she gave them a military salute. Trying to be funny kept her mind off the seriousness of what was about to happen.

Kevin ran ahead to open up the starting gate. As they walked toward it Melanie talked to Stone. "You have to run like you've never run before," she told the big bay. "Please do this for me. I love you, Stone, and I want to keep riding you, so you have to be really good for me. Do you understand?" Stone nodded his head in time with his steps, and Melanie decided to take that as his answer.

By the time Kevin had the gate open and ready for her to load, Melanie had built up her resolve. Stone would run better than ever this time. They would convince her dad to let her keep riding on the track, she told herself. Even if they didn't, at least she'd have this one last run.

Stone pranced and tossed his head, ready to go. Melanie guided him into the gate and wrapped the reins firmly around her hands, the way Ashleigh had shown her. Remembering what Naomi had said about how Stone loved to come out of the gate in a flash, she settled into the saddle, grabbing a hunk of mane and crouching low over Stone's neck. She could see Ashleigh, her father, and Uncle Mike cresting the hill. They stopped to shade their eyes against the sun. Kevin flashed her a thumbs-up, and Melanie braced herself. Out of the corner of her eye she could see Christina racing up to her dad and Mike and Ashleigh now, motioning toward the track as she talked. A moment later Melanie's dad took off, sprinting toward her. Just then Kevin hit the button. The buzzer sounded and the gate flew wide open.

Stone erupted from the gate, and Melanie leaned low to stay with him. She focused all her attention between Stone's black-tipped ears. He had the bit in his teeth, and he was running for all he was worth. Melanie didn't even try to gain control of his mouth. He had nowhere else to go but around the track, and she was going to let him do it at his own pace, even if that meant sacrificing a little control. *Don't try to boss him.* She heard Mona's voice in her head. *Be his partner.* Melanie hunkered down and let him run. If Stone wanted to blow off steam, she was going to let him do it. Ashleigh and Melanie's father were far behind now.

Melanie felt the thundering in her chest as they pounded down the track. She felt Stone's powerful shoulders rising up and down, his legs pumping, his neck stretched out long, his ears erect.

As they bolted down the backstretch Melanie saw her family gathered, black dots in the distance. She wished she could see their faces and hear what was being said. In her heart, she knew Ashleigh and Christina would be telling her dad good things. She knew now that they believed in her and would let her dad know it, too.

They rounded the turn toward home, and Melanie felt Stone hand the power back to her. He loosened his grip on the bit, and once again she made contact with his mouth. She sat back in the saddle and signaled the big bay to slow down, and he did. They dashed past the finish post at a controlled gallop that soon dropped to a canter and then a trot.

"Good boy," she called. "Good boy." Melanie patted Stone's damp neck affectionately. She circled until Stone slowed to a walk and then turned him toward the group. "We're partners, aren't we, guy?"

Melanie was in no hurry to hear what her father and Ashleigh had to say, but she couldn't put it off any longer. She couldn't even look at her father as she rode near. Ashleigh took Stone's bridle and Melanie dismounted.

Her aunt was silent as she began to lead Stone toward the group. Then Melanie spoke.

"I'm sorry, Aunt Ashleigh," she said. "I shouldn't have ridden Stone without your permission, and it will never happen again." She turned to her father as she continued. "But I had to do it. I had to show my dad that I can do this, and that I am good at this. If I hadn't disobeyed all of you, I never would have been given a chance to prove to my dad that this"—she swept her arm out over the track, and then put a hand on Stone—"and this are all I want." Melanie could no longer hold back the tears that had been burning for release all day, and she began to cry.

She swiped at her cheeks and looked up at her dad. He was frowning. "I know I had an accident with Milky Way," Melanie went on, her voice trembling. "But why can't you see that I've grown since then? I'm not a baby anymore. You have to start trusting me and my judgment someday."

Will Graham cleared his throat. He put a hand on her shoulder. "You disobeyed me," he said, "and we will have to deal with that." Melanie dropped her head, staring at her riding boots. "But I was wrong," her father added.

Melanie's head shot up.

"I shouldn't have banned you from riding without seeing how you ride these racehorses. Your aunt has done nothing but reassure me that you are a natural. Christina couldn't stop telling me how much you've given up to do this, how much you love it, how happy you've been since you started working on the track."

133

Melanie gave Ashleigh and Christina grateful looks.

"So I guess maybe I'm outnumbered," her father admitted.

Melanie sagged against Stone. It was over, and it had worked! She hugged Stone, then stepped close to her dad. "Thank you, Dad," she said softly. "I won't let you down again. I promise."

A slow smile spread over Will's face. He shook his head. "It still scares me, Mel. I won't pretend it doesn't. But I guess I'll just have to close my eyes and be proud of you. Believe me, I don't want to hold you back."

"I hate to interrupt, but you have a horse to cool out," Ashleigh said. She looked at Will. "It's part of that responsibility thing we talked about."

Will smiled and pulled Melanie close. The bear hug was a Will Graham special, and she savored every bit of it before taking Stone's reins and leading him away. Kevin followed them, smiling nonstop.

After Stone had been bathed and put away, Melanie showered and her father took her into town for lunch. Over soft tacos at the Mexicala Diner, she told him all about Pride's Perfection and how she had survived the spill of her life. "I'm still worried about Perfection," she said. "But the vet says he'll be fine."

Will shook his head and bit into a taco. "That's exactly the kind of thing I was concerned about. Even the best rider can't prevent that kind of accident."

Melanie chewed thoughtfully. "Yeah, but Dad, I could walk out of here right now and be hit by a truck. Anything can happen. No one is safe all the time. And I love riding—it's definitely worth the risk," she insisted.

"Do you really want to be a jockey one day?" her father asked.

Melanie nodded. "My father always told me I could be anything I want to."

Will groaned. "Sure! Throw my own words back at me, why don't you. I should have known they would come back to haunt me one day!"

"You've always taught me to be independent. Now you have to trust me," Melanie said.

Will nodded. "So I'm learning," he said. Then he motioned at the cherry red streak in Melanie's blond hair. "Can I trust you'll get rid of that one day?" he asked.

Melanie giggled. "Dad!"

"Don't you think the new you has matured past Kool-Aid streaks in your hair?" Will smiled, but Melanie detected a serious note in his voice.

"The hair doesn't make the woman," she quipped. "But," she went on, her voice becoming serious, "if you really want me to, I'll wash it out."

"I have a better idea. Why don't I treat you to a new hairstyle?" her father offered.

"Today? Now?" Melanie asked, startled.

"Sure! Why not?"

Melanie stuffed the last bite of her taco in her mouth and grinned. "Okay!" she agreed.

After a wash, cut, and blow-dry, Melanie's hair was shorter and bouncier. It felt springy, like somebody else's hair.

"Do you really like it?" she asked her father, patting her head, as they drove back to Whitebrook.

"For the tenth time, I love it. The question you really want to ask is, will Kevin like it?" her father said, grinning.

Melanie stopped, her hand still on her hair.

"He is your boyfriend, isn't he?" he asked.

Dad doesn't miss a trick, she thought. She almost shouted, *No!* But she refrained. "Not really," she said. "I mean, not officially." She fixed her gaze on the passing horse farms and tried to control the blush blazing on her face.

Back at Whitebrook, Melanie led her father into the broodmare barn to see Perfect Heart's baby. The filly was up and looking around, full of curiosity.

"She's got such bright little eyes," Will said softly. "And those funny white feet—she's beautiful."

"She is," Melanie agreed. "Look at those long legs," she added. "Just like her dad, Pride. They're racing legs. She's going to be a champion just like Pride, Dad. She might even win the Triple Crown one day. You never know."

Will Graham smiled and put a hand on Melanie's

shoulder. "And who will ride her to her victory?" he asked.

"Are you making fun of me, Dad?" Melanie demanded.

"No, Mel. It really might be you. I'm looking at this little filly and thinking you and she might even win the Triple Crown one day," he said, his eyes shining. "Wow. What a thought."

11

THAT NIGHT, AFTER THE OTHERS HAD RETIRED TO WATCH television or curl up with a book, Melanie wandered to the broodmare barn to meet Kevin. He was already waiting when she arrived. He leaned over the stall door. "Come and look at this, Mel!"

She hurried to see. The new filly was frolicking in circles around the mare in the big box stall, kicking up her heels. "Hard to believe she was just born this morning," Melanie said.

"Their legs get strong so quickly," Kevin said. "By next week she'll be rearing and bucking." Melanie noticed he was staring at her.

"What?" she asked self-consciously.

He touched her hair. "It really looks nice," he said, smiling.

"Oh. Thanks," Melanie said. She turned back to the

filly. "She's going to win big one day," she said.

"She might," Kevin said.

"You know," Melanie went on, "my dad didn't really want me to exercise-ride, but when he saw the baby, he said we might win the Triple Crown together one day!"

The filly pranced over to them and stretched a nose up to their hands.

"Sounds good to me," Kevin said, touching the tips of the filly's ears. "She's not afraid of us at all, is she?"

"Ashleigh and Mike said they like their foals to get used to people right away. It must be working." Melanie rubbed the filly's long face, scratching the top of her head where her forelock was only a tuft of wispy hairs. The baby shook her head comically, and pranced out of reach.

Kevin reached over to scratch the filly's withers. The filly backed up to him, and he scratched some more. When she tottered away to nurse, Kevin looked at Melanie. "Want to take a walk?" he asked.

Outside, the moon had risen, full and silvery in the sky. It was bigger than Melanie had ever seen it. They stared up at it together. "I feel like I can touch it," Melanie said, stretching out her hand.

"It's beautiful," he agreed. "Hey, why don't we take a moonlight ride instead of a walk?"

"No, Kevin. That's not a good idea." She was remembering her nighttime ride in Central Park with Milky Way.

"Aw, come on," he said. "We're out in the country, and the moon is so full it's almost daylight. Chris and I used to do it all the time when we were little." He hesitated. "We're not in the city," he reminded her. "We're safe here."

Melanie hesitated. She couldn't think of a single thing that could go wrong now that could not go wrong in broad daylight.

"You can ride Pirate. Jasper's spooky at night, so I guess I'll ride Trib. Won't that be a kick? My long legs on Trib! Heck, Pirate won't even know it's night. He can't see anyway. We'll just go out for a little while. Come on, Mel. Please?"

Melanie stared up at the dazzling silver ball hovering overhead. It was a beautiful night. "Okay," she agreed. "Let's do it!"

"Meet you at the trail in ten minutes," Kevin said, and he sprinted off to get Trib ready while Melanie headed for Pirate's stall.

Pirate whinnied at Melanie as soon as the lights came on. She rubbed his jet black neck and wiped the dust off him with a towel. A moment later she was putting the saddle pad and the saddle on. Pirate lowered his head for the bridle, prancing with anticipation.

Maybe he can't see, Melanie thought, *but he knows it's night, and he's excited about a ride.*

Kevin trotted up on Trib just as Melanie and Pirate came out of the barn. Kevin did look a little silly with his legs hanging below Trib's belly. Melanie looked out at the white fences that stretched into the night for what seemed like miles, eerily lit by moonlight. "Just a short ride," she reminded Kevin, and he nodded.

They took the trail that skirted the edge of the woods. It was so bright, it felt like daytime. Trib was docile, which was rare. "I think he's asleep," Kevin joked.

Pirate tossed his head and snorted. "This guy is wide awake," Melanie countered. The light fell across the meadow in cool streaks. It reminded Melanie of a painting. Each streak of light looked like the stroke of a brush.

Kevin rode close, his leg bumping against hers as they walked down the trail side by side and into the wildflower meadow that Melanie loved so much. Fall flowers swayed on the breeze, yellow, orange and iridescent white in the rays of moonlight. From the top of the hill, they could see the lights of the houses and barns below.

"Let's stop," Kevin suggested.

They halted their horses and Kevin reached out, taking Melanie's hand as they gazed up at the moon together. Melanie didn't want to pull away, but Pirate began to fidget and she had to take the reins in both hands.

Melanie's knees were shaking as they rode down the hill toward home. She had to fight the urge to gallop off and run like crazy across the fields, but instead she sat deeper in the saddle and sighed. *This day has been like a roller-coaster ride,* she thought as they followed the moonlit trail home. *It's been wild enough for one day.*

Ashleigh invited absolutely *everyone* to dinner the next day. She'd made two huge pans of lasagna, and had loaves of garlic bread in the oven. The smell of butter and garlic met the girls as they came in the door from school, and wafted through the house as it filled up with friends, all there to see Melanie's father before his plane took off at 10 P.M. Katie, Dylan, Cassidy, Kevin, Christina, and Melanie gathered in the living room, lounging on the floor and the couches. The first topic of conversation was Melanie's hair, and the consensus was that it looked great.

"You will still put colored streaks in it, won't you?" Katie asked. "I mean, I liked those colors. They're so you!"

"I haven't decided yet," Melanie answered.

Naomi and Samantha joined Ashleigh and Beth in the kitchen, while Mike, Will, Ian, and Samantha's husband, Tor, joined the younger set in the living room. Outside, it was raining, a light drizzle. Will sat on the couch entertaining everyone with stories and answers to all the questions about the rock groups he represented.

Melanie's mind wandered away from the conversation. She gazed out the window at the pastures that stretched along the long driveway, and the horses that grazed inside their boundaries. She'd heard about music and big stars her whole life. Those horses were what drew her, not the conversation that buzzed around her.

Kevin leaned over her. "Too much to take in?" he asked.

"I guess. I'd rather be riding or something," Melanie admitted.

Christina wandered over to the window to stand beside them. "Talking racing again?" she asked.

"I just can't believe I can ride in the morning without even worrying about it. It feels so good." Melanie shrugged.

"Dad said he'd let me ride one of the older horses on the exercise track on Saturday. Want to come watch?" Kevin asked Melanie.

"I'd love to. I think I'll be riding Stone that day, too. Naomi's going to work Faith with me," Melanie answered. She couldn't wait.

"Hey! I have a great idea. The three of us can work the horses together. It'll be like a race," Kevin suggested.

"Mom," Christina yelled before Melanie could respond.

Ashleigh came over, looking uncharacteristically domestic in her white apron over jeans and a pair of bedroom slippers. By then Christina had everyone's attention. "What's all the excitement?" Ashleigh demanded.

Naomi joined the group, her mouth full of potato chips. "What's up, guys?" she asked.

"Can we have a race Saturday on the training track?" Christina asked.

Ashleigh looked surprised. "What are you talking about, Christina?"

"Kevin said Ian was going to let him exercise one of the older horses. You're already planing to have Naomi ride Faith and Mel ride Stone. Why not make it a race? Not like a real race," she added, "but just for fun, to see how they run together. We'll all come to watch!"

Kevin looked at Ian. "Can I, Dad?"

Ian smiled. Then he shrugged. "It's okay with me," he said.

"I don't know," Ashleigh said slowly. "I don't want you guys to get the idea that this is all play. It's work. Both you and the horses need the practice," she scolded. "Besides, I don't want you to do anything dangerous."

"We won't," Melanie said. "You know I wouldn't do anything stupid, not after all this stuff with my dad." She gestured toward her father, and Will gave his daughter a smile and a thumbs-up.

Ashleigh looked at Naomi. "What do you make of all this?"

Naomi grinned. "It sounds like fun. Of course, Faith will win, but it'll be a hoot to run her with some other horses." She leveled a look at Kevin and Melanie. "I think these two can handle themselves just fine, and Stone's certainly no problem."

"All right, then," Ashleigh said. "But everyone here has to promise to come!"

"Sorry, Ash," Tor said. "I have to work Saturday."

The others promised they'd be there.

"How about you, Dad?" Melanie asked. "Do you have to go home tonight?"

Will shrugged. "Yes, but I do have all those frequent-flyer miles saved up, and I think Susan might like to see it. Maybe we can jet back."

Melanie threw her arms around her dad in a giant hug.

Ashleigh gazed around the room. "We'll plan on an early morning race Saturday," she said. She sniffed the air. "Oops, that's my garlic bread. I do believe dinner is served," she announced.

The long dining room table was full. Each person had a plate laden with lasagna and salad, and large hunks of buttered garlic bread on the side. When they had finished eating, no one wanted to move.

"I'm stuffed," Cassidy said.

"Me too," Katie added. "I can't move."

Melanie nodded in agreement. The party had been so great, but she didn't want any of her friends to leave yet. "I have an idea. Let's get out Ashleigh's old trunk and look at all her awards," she said.

Christina heard her suggestion and jumped up.

"Great idea," she said. "I haven't looked at that stuff in a long time, and you've been bugging me to get it out."

"Yes!" Cassidy said. "I've been dying to see that stuff."

"She won so many trophies," Kevin added. "They're great—especially all that stuff from when she won the Kentucky Derby and the Preakness."

Ashleigh came in from the kitchen, where she'd been loading the dishwasher. "Now what are you up to?"

"We're going to look at your old racing stuff from the attic," Christina said.

"Aw, Chris," Ashleigh said. "That's old news."

"Don't be shy, Mom," Christina teased Ashleigh. "You worked hard to make it in racing, and you should be proud of your trophies. Give me a minute, guys," Christina said, standing up as she spoke. "Mel, will you help me get it down?"

"Sure," Melanie called.

"I'll help, too," Kevin said, and the three tramped up the steps to the attic to bring down the trunk. They dragged it down into the living room, and everyone followed.

Ashleigh shook her head and disappeared back into the kitchen. But as the others opened the trunk and began pulling out her memories, she drifted into the living room and sat on the arm of the sofa watching as they passed around yellowed newspaper clippings about her wins, pictures of her in the winner's circle,

146

trophies, medals, and even her old racing silks.

"Oh, my, that was so long ago," she kept saying over and over as they pulled first one item and then another from the trunk. Melanie gazed at each clipping and photo for a long time. Ashleigh had looked exactly like Christina.

"Seems like yesterday," Mike said.

Melanie sat on the floor by Will's feet. Kevin sat beside her as Christina rooted through the trunk. Will put his hand on Melanie's shoulder. "You and Christina should both keep a trunk like this," he said, "so one day we can all sit around and look at all the trophies the two of you have won."

12

ON SATURDAY MELANIE LEFT THE HOUSE WHEN IT WAS STILL completely dark. Christina had been sleeping deeply when she passed by her bedroom door, and Melanie wondered if her cousin would wake up in time to watch the race. When she got to the barn, Faith and Stone were in crossties, waiting to go to the track for their workout. Naomi was grooming Faith, and the gray mare shook her dark mane and snorted at Stone, standing opposite her in the aisle. Just as Melanie walked up, Ashleigh emerged from the tack room with Stone's tack.

"All set to go, Mel?" Ashleigh asked.

"Sure," Melanie said. "But where's Kevin?"

"Sam and Ian just left with him," Naomi said. "He's riding old Thunder. I think Kevin's feeling a little nervous, though he'd never admit it," she added, chuckling.

148

"Can you pick out his feet?" Ashleigh asked, and handed Melanie a hoof pick. "They're having him walk Thunder for a while first to loosen up his creaky muscles and get Kevin used to the racing saddle and Thunder's huge stride. They'll meet us at the track." Ashleigh paused. "You know Kevin's riding pretty well, Mel. Do you think he'll be good at this?"

Melanie started to pick out Stone's hooves. "Kevin's good at anything he sets his mind to," she said, "especially with horses. But to tell the truth, I think he just wants to do this because I do."

"He sure is smitten with you," Naomi said.

"Smitten?" Melanie demanded. Naomi was only seventeen, but she lived with her grandmother and sometimes she sounded like a little old lady herself. "What kind of word is *smitten?*"

"Hey, leave me alone! It's one of my grandmother's favorite words, and I think it's pretty neat."

"Neat?" Melanie scoffed.

"Laugh all you want," Naomi challenged her. "Soon you'll be eating my dust, right, Faith?" she said to the pretty gray filly at her side.

"You're probably right," Melanie conceded. "But just you wait—one day I'll be hard to beat."

"Yes, you will," Ashleigh agreed as she rubbed the dust from Stone's coat with a dry towel. "But let's just take it one race at a time."

Melanie finished picking out Stone's feet and picked up the rubber saddle pad and light racing saddle. A few minutes later the big bay was tacked up and they were walking out of the barn toward the track.

Melanie was beginning to feel jittery at the thought of racing in front of an audience. "Did Dad and Susan say where they'd meet us?" she fretted.

"Susan, your dad, and Christina will all meet us at the track," Ashleigh told Melanie.

"I wish he could stay here all the time," Melanie said wistfully.

"I know," Ashleigh said.

Melanie was quiet as they walked. So much had happened in such a short time, it was almost unbelievable to her. And it had all ended up being for the best.

Melanie saw the crowd before they got to the top of the hill. Kevin was up on Thunder, a heavy-boned dark brown gelding, and Ian was holding the reins. Samantha stood beside Ian, laughing up at her pale-faced half-brother. Will and Susan, his wife, leaned on the fence side by side, with Christina, Dylan, Cassidy, and Katie standing nearby.

When Kevin saw Melanie, he waved. "We're all here for the greatest match of the century," he teased.

"It's no match," Melanie said. "According to Naomi, the winner will be Faith."

"Shhh, Mel," Kevin said. "Don't say that out loud. T-bone here thinks he has a chance."

"T-bone?" Melanie laughed.

"His name is not T-bone," Samantha scolded. "His

name is Thunder, but leave it to Kev to take away the integrity of his name."

"Let's get them in the gate," Samantha said, letting go of Thunder's reins. Kevin walked the gigantic gelding in a circle and then rode up between Stone and Faith.

"Remember what I told you, Kev," Samantha said, and stepped aside as he rode Thunder past her. "Nice and easy."

"I won't forget, boss," Kevin replied.

"Isn't the big sister always the boss?" Ian asked, a twinkle in his eyes.

All three horses loaded into the starting gate like old pros. Melanie could feel the tension boiling in Stone as he jigged in place, ready to gallop. He had not one but two horses to compete with, and his spirits were high. She glanced at Kevin and saw a drop of sweat escape from beneath his helmet and trickle down his cheek. His eyes were fixed dead ahead in nervous concentration. Melanie smiled to herself and tightened her grip on the reins. *For once Kevin is more nervous than me,* she thought. *I love it.*

When the buzzer sounded and all three horses shot out of the gate, Melanie found herself leading the pack—at least for a split second. Then Faith bounded past in a flash of gray. Melanie focused on Faith's dark tail, streaming out behind her like a flag held high, as she concentrated on catching up. She leaned low over Stone's neck and he tensed beneath her, pulling at the bit, begging to be let out a notch. *Oh, why not?* Melanie said to herself, and she gave him his head.

The big bay shot forward, eating up the dark earth beneath them and narrowing the gap behind Faith. He had almost caught up with the gray filly before his interest seemed to subside and his energy level dropped off again. Beside them, Melanie heard Thunder moving up like a freight train with the engine wide open. Kevin steered the gelding to Melanie's right, on the outside, and for a moment the three horses were almost side by side, with Faith ahead by only a neck. Melanie dug her knees in, but Stone had run himself out early, and Faith pulled ahead a length, then two. Thunder was content to stay at Stone's shoulder, and the two of them streaked past the finish line together, two lengths behind Faith.

Melanie glanced over at Kevin. He was grinning and patting Thunder's neck as he reined the gelding in. Melanie sat back and began to ask Stone to slow. Responding to her cues, he dropped to a canter and then a trot. Soon the three horses were circling back to the group.

"And in the winner's circle," Dylan called, "it's the one and only Leap of Faith, with jockey Naomi Traeger on board!"

Melanie's father began to whoop and clap, and soon everyone lining the fence was clapping and cheering along with him.

Melanie walked Stone toward them, her face split in a self-conscious grin. She wasn't disappointed at coming in second—she'd have plenty of time for winning later on. Beside her, Kevin winked playfully. "You looked good out there," he said. Kevin's face was back to its normal rosy hue, and he looked sort of cute perched up on the seventeen-hand gelding.

"You too," Melanie said.

They walked their horses back to the barn, and everyone trailed along, laughing about the race and how much fun it had been.

"Next time you'll come in first," Melanie's father assured her.

"Not so fast," Kevin called. "She'll have me to contend with—I think I'm going to want to do more of this."

Will Graham raised his eyebrows and shot Melanie a knowing look. Melanie blushed and looked away.

Ashleigh was ahead of everyone on the trail, talking to Samantha. She turned around, walking backward. "Don't forget that the yearling sale is tonight," she reminded the rest of the group. "You are all invited to come along in the Whitebrook van."

"I wouldn't miss it," Dylan remarked, nudging Christina. Melanie saw her cousin's cheeks redden.

"I'll be there," Kevin replied.

Will shook his head. "Sure wish we could make it," he said. "But we could only take two days off work, I'm afraid. We'll have to be on that plane tonight."

"The life of a big-time record producer," Susan said with a mock grimace. Then she laughed, and Will squeezed her waist.

"I can't make it, either. Gram and I are playing cards with her friends tonight," Naomi said. "Maybe next time."

Cassidy looked at Katie. "Want to ride with me? My dad wants to go, so we could pick you up. We could meet everyone over there," she offered.

Katie pushed back a long strand of blond hair. "Sounds good to me," she said.

Will reached over to touch Stone's neck. "I see why you like it here so much," he said in a voice only Melanie could hear. "But just for the old man, promise me again that you'll be careful?"

Melanie looked up into his eyes as they walked along. "I promise," she said solemnly.

By three o'clock Will and Susan had left and Melanie was helping to load up Whitebrook's big horse van. The auction wouldn't begin until six, but Ashleigh believed in arriving early so that the horses could settle in. Plus the first ones there got the best stalls.

One by one Kevin and Mike led the four yearlings out of the barn.

"Thanks for helping me with these guys," Mike said. "If you hadn't been around to practice loading them, we'd be having a ton of trouble right now."

"Well, I gave them grain every time I loaded them," Kevin admitted.

"You did what?" Mike asked with a laugh.

"It was just a handful, but it worked," Kevin said.

Dylan and Christina grinned. "Only you would think of that, Kevin," Dylan said. "Food always works for you!"

Ashleigh laughed, too. "You have a point there," she said. "But we'd better not let them down this time. We want them in a good mood for the sale," she added. Melanie went to get a few scoops of sweet feed, and as the young horses were led into the van, she fed them a handful of grain.

"So how did you decide which ones to sell?" Melanie asked, remembering Ashleigh's earlier indecision.

"I never want to lose any of them, but I'm selling a few more than I'd first thought. I think we have a better crop coming next year," Ashleigh said.

"You have Heart's baby," Melanie reminded her.

"It's too soon to tell, but I have a good feeling about her, too," Ashleigh agreed.

When they arrived at Keeneland, Mike and Ashleigh were directed by security to drive to the back of the barn to unload the horses. As soon as the van stopped, Ashleigh jumped out.

"Why don't you kids go inside, where it's warmer?" she said. "Mike and I can handle these guys."

The sale arena was round, with a sawdust floor and

155

a shiny wooden railing. The seats surrounding it were tiered like bleachers in a stadium, but each chair was cushioned, like in a movie theater. The horses would be led in by their handlers from a side door, and walked and jogged around for the buyers to see. The auctioneer would sit on a platform inside the ring, with two assistants beside him who would scan the crowd for bids, and a recorder who would write down the details of each sale.

Within an hour the place would be teeming with people, but it was still early and only scattered handfuls of people gathered among the seats and in the aisles around the ring. Melanie had thought she and Christina, Dylan, and Kevin might be the only young people there, and she was right. There were a lot of older people, all dressed in expensive-looking coats and hats. Then she recognized one couple.

"It's the snobby set," Melanie whispered, pointing out Lavinia and Brad Townsend across the ring. She looked for their son, Parker, but he was nowhere in sight. Parker's grandfather, Clay Townsend, was a nice man and a good friend to Ashleigh, but Parker's father and mother were another story altogether.

"I wonder where Katie and Cassidy are," Christina said.

"We wonder, too."

The voices behind Melanie made her jump, but she realized almost right away that it was Katie and Cassidy. "Hey, guys, you made it!"

"Did you have any doubt?" Cassidy asked, tucking her blond hair behind her ears. "Scoot over."

Christina laughed. "With you two, we never know," she said. "Come on. The bidding won't start for a while—let's go check on our yearlings."

"Okay," Melanie agreed, and jumped up from her seat.

"Sounds good," Kevin said. "I can see if Sam's here yet. She and Tor are bringing the trailer, in case anything looks promising."

They found Mike leaning against stall door number thirty-one. He was talking to a prospective buyer. Ashleigh was inside the stall, grooming the tall chestnut yearling they called Ringo. Melanie leaned over the stall door. "Want any help?" she offered.

"No, thanks," Ashleigh said. "This keeps my mind off the sale. Go have fun. Take a look at what's out there. Sam's shopping for Whisperwood," she added. "You can give her a hand."

Before he could do it, Melanie took Kevin's hand. He flashed her a surprised grin. Then Dylan reached for Christina's hand and the four of them walked down the long shed row, looking in on each horse.

Kevin almost ran right into Samantha as she rounded the corner into the center aisle. "Watch where you're going, little brother," she said. Then she took a step back when she saw the rest of the group. "Well the gang's all here," she remarked, smiling.

"Find anything?" Melanie asked.

"Yep—come and tell me what you think," Sam said.

The group followed Samantha down the row of stalls until she stopped at the last one. Melanie peered in. Inside, a tall gray filly with square knees and feet as big as saucers stood quietly pulling hay from her hay net.

Katie whistled. "Wow! She's a big one."

"She's out of the same line as Finn," Samantha said, referring to her big Irish Thoroughbred stud. "They have the same grandsire and they're bred for jumping—so she'd be perfect for us," she said excitedly. "Tor's still looking. She's a little expensive, but I think I've found what I want!"

"Look at that face," Christina said. "She's so big you'd think she'd be sort of gawky-looking or something, but she's really pretty."

Melanie agreed. The filly had a pure white star on her dark gray forehead and a pink snip on her nose. Her forehead was broad and her nose slender, almost like an Arabian. "You only like her because she's dark gray, like Sterling," Melanie teased Christina.

The group left Samantha behind and spent the next ten minutes looking at one yearling after another. Some were built and bred for racing, while others were potential hunters. A few might bring a high price because of their lineage, though it was too early to tell how they would run. Others had conformation that showed they'd never amount to much on the track. They would make better pleasure horses if they were given the chance, but Melanie knew that was unlikely. They would be bought cheap and raced for a short time, until their owners gave up on them and sold them again.

Melanie saw Ashleigh and Mike watching a tall man trot out a chestnut filly with four white socks and a tag with the number 42 pasted to her rump. They weren't supposed to be buying, but they must have found one they liked.

Cassidy touched Melanie's sleeve. "I think it's about time to get inside if we're going to get seats," she said. "The auction's going to start soon."

Melanie looked around. The aisle was crowded all of a sudden, and the air buzzed with whinnies and voices. "I guess you're right," she agreed, and followed the others out of the barn and into the auction area.

The auctioneer was seated on the platform, making notations on a clipboard. They found six seats together in one of the back rows.

"There's Ashleigh and the others," Cassidy said, and pointed to a group of seats up front near the doors where the yearlings would be brought in.

The auctioneer took the microphone and welcomed everyone to the eighty-fifth annual Keeneland Acres Thoroughbred yearling sale. Then they watched the yearlings come into the ring one by one. Most of them had never been off the farms where they were born and were wide-eyed with terror, rolling their eyes

159

at the wall of people surrounding them. One dull-coated chestnut colt walked around the ring complacently, head hung low. His eyes were glassy and he paid no attention to the crowd.

"Do you think he's been drugged?" Melanie asked.

"Probably," Christina said.

The next yearling was a leggy black filly that pranced and bucked and reared. "Wow, that one is wild," Kevin remarked.

"She just needs to be worked with," Melanie said as she watched the filly's antics.

"Melanie knows her stuff," Kevin joked, and Melanie threw him a mock dirty look.

The next one out was number forty-two, the filly Ashleigh and Mike had been looking at. As her handler jogged her around the ring at a trot, she lifted her delicate legs and tossed her head. The bids began at fifteen thousand. Melanie saw Ashleigh raise her number twice, then it was over and the auctioneer's gavel came down with a bang. "Sold for twenty-five thousand dollars to number twelve!" the auctioneer cried.

Melanie strained her eyes to see her aunt's number.

"Mom is number twelve!" Christina shouted excitedly, and Melanie gave her a high five. Another beautiful chestnut for Whitebrook!

Samantha's gray filly trotted out two yearlings later. Melanie heard Cassidy suck in her breath. She was amazing. How could something so big-boned and tall be so graceful?

"Awesome," Melanie whispered.

Christina shook her head, looking grim. "She's going to go sky high," she said.

"Man, I hope not. Sam never gets the horse she picks out," Kevin said, shaking his head.

The bidding started at six thousand and went up fast. When it went over ten thousand, Kevin looked at his lap and shook his head again. "That's more than Samantha will spend," he told them sadly. But Samantha was staying in, a look of grim determination on her face.

"Sold for fifteen thousand, five hundred dollars, to number twenty-two," the auctioneer called, and Kevin's head flew up again. "Who got her?" he demanded.

"Samantha!" Melanie cried, and jabbed him in the arm. "Your sister's tougher than you are," she joked.

"All right!" Kevin whooped. Across the arena Lavinia Townsend glared at them, and Melanie giggled.

On the ride home Melanie sat close to Kevin in the truck. She felt so happy. Perfection was healing faster than anyone had expected. The vet said the colt might be laid up for less than the six months he'd predicted, and it looked like Perfection would make a full recovery. In the meantime Melanie could ride Stone and Pirate, and maybe even the new chestnut filly when she was big enough. She and Christina were finally back to being friends, and having a guy friend like

Kevin was like icing on a double chocolate cake.

Melanie closed her eyes and dozed. In her dream she saw Perfect Heart's filly, but in the fuzzy outline of sleep the newborn was a full-sized three-year-old Thoroughbred, standing in the winner's circle at Churchill Downs as cameras flashed all around. From the filly's back, Melanie smiled for the reporters, wearing Whitebrook's blue and white racing silks.

The van bounced over a bump and Melanie opened her eyes. *It was just a dream*, she thought, *but one day it will come true!*

LOIS SZYMANSKI couldn't have a pony when she was young, so she dreamed up stories about horses and ponies and put them on paper. Years later, she is still writing stories about horses and ponies. This is her ninth horse book for young readers. She and her family own three horses: a half-crazy half-Arab mare called Christa, a Chincoteague pony stallion named Sea Feather (purchased at the Chincoteague Wild Pony Swim and Auction), and his first filly, Ellie.

THOROUGHBRED

If you enjoyed this book, then you'll love reading all the books in the THOROUGHBRED series!

At bookstores everywhere,
or call 1-800-331-3761 to order.

HarperCollins*Publishers*
www.harpercollins.com

THOROUGHBRED

All books are
$4.50 U.S./$5.50 Canadian